The Slow Tide
of Nightfall

Books by Stewart Moore

Dandelions Have Their Own Gold Standard
For Nought / Mr. Mankind: Two One-Act Plays
Over the Hill to the Moorehouse

STEWART MOORE

The Slow Tide of Nightfall

CRANBERRY TREE PRESS
WINDSOR, ONTARIO, CANADA

Cranberry Tree Press
5060 Tecumseh Rd. E., Suite 173
Windsor, Ontario, Canada N8T 1C1

Flight 210 previously published in *The Fiddlehead*, summer 1987,
no. 152. *It Could Be The Ocean* previously published in *Waves*,
Spring 1987, vol. 15, no. 4. *The Slow Tide of Nightfall* published in
The University of Windsor Review, 1989, vol. 22, no. 1.

Cover photo by David Stewart Moore.

Printed in Canada.

05 04 03 02 01   5 4 3 2

Canadian Cataloguing in Publication Data

Moore, Stewart, 1919–1997
    The slow tide of nightfall

ISBN 1-894668-00-6

    1. Fathers and sons—Fiction. I. Title.

PS8576.O6158S59 2000   C813'.6   C00-900995-7
PR9199.3.M624S59 2000

For my mother
Mabel Apps Moore Morgan
and my son
David Stewart Moore.

Foreword

During our frequent walks, Stewart and I often discussed his writing. It was always his dream to see his stories published, but that didn't happen during his lifetime. Stewart had often said to me, "Well, my part is to do the writing," and after his death it became apparent that my part is to see that these stories are published.

My thanks go to many people. To Fred Wallace, for his invaluable computer assistance over the years. To Dr. Alistair MacLeod and to Mr. Michael Dunwoody of the University of Windsor for their encouragement and the helpful suggestions they made to Stewart. To David Stewart Moore, who shared his father's dreams. To Lenore Langs who said, "Yes, I will look at Stewart's stories," and has continued looking patiently and steadily so that these stories can be in print.

And always, my thanks to Stewart.

HELEN MOORE

Contents

The Last Halloween

HE WAS in no mood for comedy when he came in the door from work that day and saw me sprawled on the kitchen floor. I'd had the pumpkin in my hands, and when I fell it pitched forward to smash just inside the door. My father stepped over the mess and stood in front of me. I was still sitting on the floor, with my curling black mustache partially unglued on the left side and a black derby tilted rakishly on my head.

The fall rains have gone now and the snow has not yet come. It is the quiet time after Indian summer before the winter sets in. It is the end of October and it is Halloween.

At this season every year, I think of that Halloween fifteen years ago, and there is a deep aching for my father. I wish I could set down what happened that night and find the solace that has eluded me these years. I am not sure I can do that truly, as truly as I must if I am to be free of the ache I have always felt for that last Halloween, and for my father going into the November storms with the last day of October weighing heavily upon him.

Since that day Halloween has haunted me. It does not come black-caped and hooded with an eerie whistling through the darkness. There is no witchcraft at all, no conjuring up the supernatural. It is all very ordinary, but extraordinarily painful.

It had been a difficult year. Mother had died the previous December after a long illness. She had hoped to live past Christmas, not "spoil it" for father and me, but it was not to be. I am sorry I was responsible for spoiling Halloween as well. It would have been better had I stopped going out Halloween nights.

The year before, my friends and I had decided it would be our last Halloween to trick or treat.

"We're too big to go out trick or treatin'," Tom said. I suggested we just go out and kibitz the other kids on the street.

"No, let's have a Halloween party. Have the kids on the block over in our basement." That was Carl's idea. Tom and Carl were twins, and we three were inseparable. But the Bartons moved away in August, and there was no party.

Years earlier my father had been gloomy when I gave up Santa Claus. It seemed a personal loss to him. So he was determined to keep the Halloween ritual going another year. When I was very small, he had gone out with me Halloween nights, walking along the sidewalk, watching me cross the streets. And now, for this last Halloween he wanted to go out with me again.

"I'll put on an old hat and jacket," he said, "and I've

got a beard I didn't have last year. I won't go up to the doors with you, but I'll walk along the sidewalk. Not as much fun as with Tom and Carl, but one more year, eh?" I was not too keen on going out, but it seemed to mean so much to my father that I decided to do it one more time.

In thinking of this every year, I try to understand what had happened that day in my father's life before he came into the kitchen and saw me with that mess on the floor. It helps me if I remember that there were other mishaps in his day that played a part in his upset and in what eventually came of that Halloween.

He must have seen jack o'lanterns on his way to work and coming home that day, carved from pumpkins and with smiles or frowns, round or jagged or triangle eyes, and mouths that opened on the candles inside. And there were cut-outs and pictures on the school-room windows he passed going to and from work, pictures of ghosts and goblins and witches on broom sticks.

He was a little late coming from work that night, so he would already have passed some of the younger kids out on the sidewalks, going from door to door with their high-pitched chant, "trick or treat!" There were a few who still called out the older line, "help the poor!" and all of them had shopping bags large enough to hold the candy and gum, popcorn balls and apples they gathered.

Some fool (the word was my father's) not looking where he was driving, going well beyond the speed limit, bumped into the back of my father's car on his way home from work. Earlier in the day the boss had asked my father for the monthly reports a week ahead of time. He'd had a hard day.

I didn't know any of this at the time my father walked through the door and saw me on the kitchen floor. I had finished carving a face on the pumpkin and was taking it to the side porch to light a candle in it. I fell on some of the slippery seeds on the kitchen floor.

I didn't have a shirt on, my pants were cut-offs on top of khaki slacks with a green belt, and I had on the old derby hat. I looked like something from a Laurel and Hardy movie, but my father didn't find it the least bit funny.

In trying to write this truly, I find these words just don't match the tone I want to capture in telling about that day. Nothing is false and yet the whole has a fraudulent ring to it, as if the description holds the experience up to ridicule or laughter rather than regret.

In the years since, I have often wished that a Halloween wizard had waved a magic wand over my father at that catastrophic moment, and turned back the clock ten minutes. That my father had been outside the door again, I had cleaned up the mess and composed myself and had a cup of hot tea ready for him, and he had come in again and everything had been all right on what was to be my last Halloween.

But there was no Halloween wizard, no magic. My father did not go out the door and come in again. He hollered at me for my clumsiness, for the mess on the kitchen floor where I'd dropped the pumpkin, and the garbage on the counter where I'd carved it. I in turn retreated into self-conscious sulking. Then he tried to order me to shape up and get ready so we could leave. He saw that wouldn't work, and so he tried pleading, cajoling, joshing, and joking.

"Please get ready now so we can go out. *Please.*"

He tried again. "I'm not dressed for Halloween begging, but I do beg of you, get ready."

And again. "Hey, maybe if I put on a bum's old hat and pants I could beg you to go out with me, eh?"

I soon realized how much it meant to him, that he was sorry he had hollered at me for the mess on the floor, for not being ready to go out trick or treating. But I went sulking off to my room and closed the door.

He probably knew there was a good possibility I would not be going out for Halloween at all. That eventually I would come around, but it would be the next day or next week, surely not in time to go out that night, Halloween night. When that hit him he came to my room, contrite, pleading with me to get ready and go out. By then I had changed from the Halloween clothes I had on, and was back in my jeans.

I don't know if I sensed it then or if I am reading this back into it years later; but it did seem that something was being cast in cement, and that if I didn't soon do something it would forever be too late. I had a similar feeling when my high school class was going to Quebec City and for some reason long forgotten I was too stubborn to go. I sensed even at the time that I would regret it. Every time I go to Quebec City now, I feel something there is hidden from me, something I will never find.

Perhaps the reason my father was so intent on going

out that night had to do with some last Halloween he'd had years earlier. He might have been struggling – as I am now – to redeem from pain some long-past experience. Or perhaps he didn't want to spoil my last Halloween, didn't want it to be a bad memory, realized the opportunity might be lost for us to go out together one more time. He was fighting, I think, against one more loss to the many he'd already suffered in his life.

I wouldn't budge. I wasn't going out unless I felt good about it. When he saw this finality, it was all he could do to keep from losing his temper and hollering at me all over again.

"Come on now, that's enough sulking and stalling. Let's go!" He wanted somehow to be able to drive me to get ready and go out, but the more he raised his voice, the more I retreated. He was afraid to let it go, wanting to do everything in his power to change my mind; yet he knew that his efforts were only alienating me further. So the last Halloween ended. There would be no chance to make it right. It had happened, and as quickly as it happened it was too late to do anything about it but grieve.

That last Halloween the doorbell sounded every few minutes or so, and my father handed out candy and peanuts. He could not even interest me in doing that. At first I wouldn't come out of my room. Eventually I did come out when I recognized some of the voices at our door and my dad chatting as he gave out goodies. I wonder if he was finding some satisfaction in the other kids that he had been denied in me.

Gradually I moved around the edge of the living

room, finally sitting down to watch the kids at the door. I saw the big bags of candy they had, and the kids with pillowcases bulging. For a brief moment I wished that I could be younger again – and going along the streets with Tom and Carl. I wondered where they were and if they were out begging or if they were having their party.

At about ten-fifteen my dad turned off the porch light. I thought that if he had asked me at that moment to go out, that I would have jumped at the opportunity. He didn't ask me, of course, and I know I would have refused anyhow. We both wanted very badly to salvage the evening, but unfortunately we did not know how to get out of the way and let it happen.

All of this happened fifteen years ago, as I said. It has helped me to set it down and realize there were factors other than my own clumsiness and sulkiness involved. My father surely had his part in it, and so did events of earlier that day, as well as losses stemming from the Christmas before. Even allowing for all of this, the aching is only slightly lessened.

I have a daughter of my own now. Kathy is almost a year old, and I look forward to her first Halloween in a year or so. I believe in starting her young. The last Halloween will come soon enough.

It occurs to me that my father could be somewhere along the sidewalk when Kathy and I go out trick or treating. Perhaps he will be dressed as a spirit, invisible of course, walking with us. We will leave that invisible space open for him.

It could happen. It's the time of witches and magicians, and mostly the time of spirits. My father would be a natural for it. The authentic spirit costume, invisible, on this first Halloween.

Zinty Tinty

THEY TALKED to Dane even though they were barely speaking to each other, and he listened although it tore him.

"He leaves the door open," his Mother said, "and I see him through two mirrors, playing with himself, your father. He grunts and groans and has that look on his face." Years earlier his father had told Dane it caused the pimples on his cousin Ted's face and would lead to insanity if Ted kept doing it.

"She used a big diaphragm, your mother, and I was always bumping into it. Now she doesn't even want to be a wife to me anymore. *Then* it was the bumper and *now* it's nothing at all."

As they drew farther from each other, they tried to pull Dane closer to them. He heard them both but what was he to do? Their words cut across his ears. As soon as he could he went into another room and held his head. The pain sliced through him.

His father bumping into the diaphragm, mother

being laid on and bumped into, the sweat and groans and heavy breathing; and wondering where the man went, the kindly man she married. And his father, pushed beyond the tenuous limits of tenderness into the maelstrom of unbridled passion, learning to despise himself and his love. What had been tender desire and soft words, grew and became the white heat of passion that threatened to consume him. Rapture became ravenous and rapacious. That part of him defiled, desecrated, tore him asunder and yet brought moments of ecstacy, something beyond him: a pull from the realm of the species and having such power over him.

And Dane wondering, knowing there was something else, something evil, dirty, not for his eyes or ears. Not wanting either one to hurt the other or be hurt. The arguments, the tension, the pain. And nothing he could do about it. Living so distantly in such close quarters. Wondering why it came to him now in such savage turmoil if not from the depths of the primal scene of his childhood. He had been witness to it, yet was certain of nothing, it having happened when he was too young to block it out, when it came as whispers or groans in the night, and the sound of bedsprings – "yes, yes, that's it, I did hear it, it's not make-believe!" – and he had not known its insidious impact on him until now.

* * *

His father climbed to the highest point inside the house, where the rafters met the ridgeboard in the unfinished attic. On the rafters there he wrote his predictions, what Dane would become: his father's way of shouting from the housetops his confidence in him. For years he wrote, never telling Dane, superstitious that telling would put a hex on it.

One day, emboldened by Dane's achieving so much of what he had foretold on the rafters, his father said, "I saw your numbers on the rafters, high up by the ridge-board."

"Oh, those. I didn't write them while I was away up there. I was on the ground when I did it, working with the rafters on the saw horses. I had a job figuring it out, the rafter angles, using the square." It was when Dane was building the house, when he was nineteen.

"That's why it's important to go as far as you can in school. I've always had trouble in the shop with my math, having to figure things out the long way." His father would tell him then about school in Glasgow and how he had to drop out, took his apprentice training there. "I learned tool and die-making the right way, not like the die barbers over here." Telling how tough the teachers were in "the old country," and their ferocity in disciplining students.

"If I was in trouble at school and got a caning for it, when I got home there was a threshing waiting for me." Dane could understand that. His grandfather was a bruiser of a man.

"I wrote my predictions beside your numbers." His father was talking about the rafters again. "From corporal to sergeant to sergeant-major. Then the leftenants, second and first." He always pronounced it "leftenant".

"I skipped sergeant-major, went right to second lieutenant. But you didn't get the private in there, Dad, twenty-one dollars a day – once a month. I think I'm proudest of that one, like K.P., kitchen police, just surviving it."

"It was silly of me to be superstitious all these years. Nothing could have stopped you, nothing ... except ... that woman." His father always referred to her as "that woman" except the time he seemed to align with her against Dane and his mother. Dane was twenty-four by then, just before his divorce.

And then abruptly his father stopped and wrote no more on wood. He began to write more privately, in a finely cramped hand, in the diaries he later left for Dane. On the rafters or in his diary, he always used a soft No. 2 pencil, whittling away at it with his pocket knife to keep it to a fine point.

After high school Dane got a job operating a fork lift truck in a warehouse. In his spare time he read a lot about carpenter work and house-building. Whenever he saw a house being built, he would stop and watch and ask questions. Someday he wanted to build his own house in the country. He looked at farms and acreage and finally bought a half-acre.

He spent week-ends there clearing the tall grass, planting fruit trees, taking the sod off and spading a garden. In the fall he built a small shop, a place to keep his tools and mower, and he strung a hammock inside or out when he wanted to sleep over. He got some part-time carpentry jobs, week-ends, learning the trade and saving his extra money.

When his father walked out one day after an argument with his mother, Dane took a three-week vacation, bought lumber and supplies, hired a part-time carpenter to help him, and roughed in the house. It was a story and a half, the half being the attic. That was when he put the numbers on the rafters, trying to figure out rafter angles to saw.

Dane thought the house he was building had something to do with his father coming back. He'd told Dane's mother it was the final separation. When the house was enclosed, his mother gave up the apartment in the city and moved in with him.

His father was soon driving by the house he was building, then stopping to help with the siding and wiring, and finally moving in once it was completed. Within a year Dane was in the army and his father wrote the predictions on the rafters.

* * *

His parents' separation was just one of many. It seemed they were arguing all through his childhood. It tore him apart because he loved them both.

When Dane was about five, and was startled out of his sleep at night by their arguing in the kitchen, he would sneak out of his bed and hide under the dining room table, among the chairs. He felt very small and very alone crouched there. His older brother, Harry, always seemed to sleep through the arguments and never mentioned them the next day.

He had to be at closer range than his bedroom, fearing the loud voices might lead to more than shouting.

They never did, but his fears did not lessen. He had to be on hand if any fighting started, to come between them, keep them from blows.

Years later he thought that each of them had been in the grip of whatever the other was to be protected from. The impending violence seemed to be as foreign and threatening to one as to the other. They seemed to be transported for the moment into entirely different persons.

And then there were the silences. From his bed he wouldn't have known what was happening then. Only from his advance outpost under the dining room table could he hear what was happening and be ready to jump in.

The endings perplexed Dane. Sometimes they would be quiet a while and then embrace and go to bed where he heard other, muffled, noises, at times as disturbing as the earlier ones. On other occasions his father threw his things in a suitcase and walked out.

When Dane heard the door slam, he would come out of hiding. "I don't know what we're going to do," his mother would say then. "There's a gas bill due, and the house payment in a week." One time, Dane tried to get a paper route to earn some money, but the manager told him he was too young.

And then his father would come back, in a day or two or a week. In later years Dane read in the diary that his father was devastated by these separations, missed his mother very much and was always anxious to get back. "Ate alone, then by myself to the hotel. From the time I leave work until the next day I don't talk to anyone. Plenty of time to think. I love Moms and miss her."

*   *   *

Bedtime was always a time of happy rituals for Dane and his father. When he was about six, his father would sit on the edge of Dane's bed and ask him, "Where did you think of me today?" Dane would remember he had been cutting through a field to see a robin's nest, or he was having fig newtons and milk after school. And then his father would tell him where he had thought of Dane: eating a tomato for his lunch or at his bench working on a new die for an automobile tail light. It couldn't just be "oh, during the afternoon" or "at school" or "at the shop" but had to be very specific, as if the concrete details clinched it into something real that would never be forgotten.

There were nursery rhymes and songs, one of the favourites being a nonsense rhyme his father had learned as a child in Scotland: "Zinty Tinty figger dee fell, El Dell dromma nell, Herky Perky torey rope, On ton tuesy jope." He never knew what it meant.

When he was about fifteen, it was important to him to get books for his father whenever he went to the library for a school assignment. "See if you can get me a book on a criminal courtroom trial, or a fraud investigation, or a spy story. That last one was good." His father often talked about what he was reading, and their idea of Dane's being a trial lawyer grew during this time. It was his father's idea before his.

15

Many of his father's predictions about Dane came true, and his father wrote on. And then he stopped telling Dane what he was writing, disappointed, Dane thought, about what his son was doing. The father never said it in so many words, but Dane could feel his disapproval. After Dane had been in the army three years and married "that woman," his father stapled insulation between the rafters and covered them with paneling.

"I wrote on the rafters that you would 'play the field' rather than get married." Dane realized his father'd written it for his sake, wanting him to have a social life without becoming tied down. "Marriage changes and we are changed by it," his father said. There was first a nostalgic and then a bitter tone to his voice.

Even after Dane married, he continued to climb the ladder of accomplishments his father had predicted for him: his final promotion to Captain. But it was not the same for his father. Dane could see that now, but he didn't at the time. He had not looked in time at the rafters before they were covered.

Dane suspected his father had lost interest in his life. He felt small and insignificant, so different from earlier years when he proudly carried his father's ideals and ambitions into action in life, with his father not just the bystander, but the one whose teaching and support and constant predictions of success spurred Dane on.

"Why did you do it? Why didn't you do it? Why did you build the house rather than go to university right then? Why did you refuse to go to law school? Why did you get married to that slut, pissing your life down the sewer, letting her unhitch your wagon from the star and hitch it to her bedpost? Why didn't you make good on all that promise? Such a waste! Why didn't you become a trial lawyer, a holy terror in the courtroom — (he rolled his r's on that one) — a champion of the under-dog? My God, the brain, the most important instrument in the world, and you let yours rot and idle to death, as-phyxiated by the carbon monoxide of your own brain idling! What a waste! Why did you? Why didn't you?"

His father didn't, of course, say a word of it to Dane, yet he could hear every syllable reverberating off the auditory receptors of his own guilt. He didn't miss one beat or breath of it. It sounded and resounded. Because, of course, Dane thought he would finally read it in his father's diaries.

The diaries were among the few things left for Dane when his father died. He was anxious to read them, an-ticipating that he might read some criticisms of his falling away from the life his father had envisioned for him, especially his mistake in the marriage. But Dane saw very little beyond a few references to "that woman." He also wondered if there was anything about his father's stays at the hotel, when he left home during the separations. Dane remembered being suspicious after seeing *Death of a Salesman*, Willy Loman and his woman at the hotel. Some nights Dane would waken from a dream about the hotel, get up and go to the di-aries again. His father's writing was so small, he thought perhaps he had missed something on previous readings, that something was hidden among the very fine words. Each time he found nothing more than he had read earlier.

"Shopped for odds and ends, toilet articles I need when I'm away from Moms. May get a little radio for the hotel room."

"Had my dinner at Rheaums. It's hell eating alone. Sitting out front of the hotel after dinner, until dark. Listening to the conversation. They all talk so big to each other, but once inside their rooms I bet it's as boring and empty as mine."

There were no predictions in the diary, no lofty ambitions cited, no future foretold. Only the humdrum happenings of the day just ended. The sadness, the loneliness, the frustration of not knowing what to do. Unhappy alone, away from Moms, but not knowing how to resolve that, fearing to go back to the same life, and then separate again. Each time it took more out of him.

But, by God, it's taken a lot out of me too. Always trying to protect Mom when they fought, support her when he left, never all that free to do what I wanted, and then always he came back and threw me off again. Pulled and torn between them. Loving them both but jarred by the noises of bedsprings and cursing and trying to believe the soft words that followed – or did they come before? And what has all of this done to poor Mother!

When his father had to drop out of school, his ambitions and dreams must have disappeared, only to grow and die yet again when Harry dropped out and disappointed him. Dane thought that in the postponment and shifting of his father's dreams, they had grown more insistent, and they were even more precise by the time they finally came to rest on Dane. He was going to be a trial lawyer. He carried this vision for many years.

Dane looked backwards to the bedtime rituals with his father, to the quicksand shifting of his father's goals from himself to Harry, to the way he gathered his hopes and regrouped them to rest in Dane. Again he could look forward and he was not disheartened for a long time. Then the life Dane wanted for himself collided with the vision his father had for so many years nurtured for him. In that collision Dane veered off and it was never the same again. It was as if Dane had abandoned his father, and all that he had accomplished was forgotten, was nothing.

Dane married "that woman" and decided to work with his hands, to pick up hammer and saw rather than law books.

In his military days, Dane carried to fulfillment most of his father's prophecies. He brooded that his father didn't always know the obstacles he had to overcome. That, for example, his final promotion to Captain hinged on getting along as Adjutant of the most bitterly demanding full-chicken colonel in the service.

But after the army, Dane didn't go on to university. He knew his father felt it was a waste, but Dane wanted to build houses and that's what he did. Ironically, his father had given Dane both the confidence and the immediate reason and need for building his first house.

Dane thought it might eventually have happened – his father's disappointment – even had he not married, or not married someone so wrong for him. He surely was no longer the boy of his father's dreams. He had come to nurture dreams of his own. They paralleled, for a while, the course of his father's goals, and then in time they diverged.

So many forces warred within Dane. His parents' fighting had a devastating impact on him. He sometimes wondered if it was that childhood experience which led him, even if unconsciously, to choose a mate who too willingly helped him repeat the strifes of his parental home. Further, his parents' conflicting aspirations for him confused and tore him: mother for security and routine and father for risk and adventure. He did have thoughts of going to university, or moving out on his own, away from his parents. Perhaps he overestimated his importance to them, to his own and their detriment. But when he saw the chance to build the house he wanted, and to provide a home for his separated mother at the same time, he did not hesitate. And then his father came back. The pattern kept repeating: leaving and returning, and each time Dane had to shift, to try and accommodate changing goals and feelings. Eventually Dane took up his own vision in the hope that it would remain steady whether his father stayed or left.

I grieve these opposing camps that continue to war within me. Yet surely I provided them sanctuary through those years I've been unable to turn aside either my mother or my father and the conflicting needs I felt from them.

His father wouldn't say anything to upset Dane. What was the use? It was too late for that. Too late to do anything about predictions unfulfilled. Let them sink into oblivion, all the dreams and prophecies. They are covered, mercifully now, by paneling, and new owners of the house will walk under them unmindful of their hidden presence. No one will know. In time the oblivion will be complete.

Dane had been out of the army several years, divorced and living on his own, when his mother and father separated for the last time, and Dane heard he had gone to the same hotel. He called there to see him. He had been taken to the hospital with terminal cancer. Dane visited him several times a week.

Time has passed and Dane has settled into a type of work that keeps him close to rafters and the possibility of marking predictions there.

He takes pride in working with his hands, building homes where people can live and raise a family. High on the rafters he writes on each house he builds: "You'll have a happy home: ZT-HP." Nobody notices his writing or has ever asked him what ZT-HP stands for. It's his way of bringing his father into what he's doing, even if he isn't a trial lawyer in the courtroom. His father would know who Zinty Tinty and Herky Perky are, and be glad to join them in the prediction.

Rosie

BACK THROUGH the wife-lost hours of it, he went down into the thickened night. He had wakened heavily wet, struggling from some now grim now fair scene and her in it cooing shrieking lashing and then heavy breathing gasping, and always caring altar caring for his whimtokens of need, taking loaves and fish for five thousand for his parched open mouth. But she was gone, nine years gone down the conduit of death, and the time gone too and now he looked to the windowed wall where no light pierced and no air breathed to this once shared bed and room where her slips and hose and nightgown and fragrance still lingered and lay on him uneasily scentdrawn to love and indifference and bitterness unresolved in the stillbound nights.

He had tried to sleep downstairs but felt the falling of her above him, and for days he could not look into the bedroom again, but then, in a morbid-like stirring, lashed his fears and desires and bound himself to what lurked and then leaped beyond him and he was stilled.

He thought then that he would go, he would visit his son this day. No stars or moon outlined the window beside his loneslept bed taut on the wide pineboard floor, but he knew that time would lighten the caved recesses in the long deep shadow we call night.

The large shadow would recede and he would curl his blanket aside then and look through the glass to the smaller shadows inked and drawn out of the ground by the rising sun, caricatures of the posts and trees and barn they mimicked and hid behind: Siamese-twinned, tethered at the base, unable to flee that, but stretching out and shrinking back as the sun moved. He turned over in bed and there was no sound but the pine floor creak under the casters as he turned. He would go to his son's this day and he slept on that.

Going down the stairs he looked at pictures of his wife, eye level above each step, from their wedding picture down through the years to the last, the one now turned to the wall, of her in the casket with corsage, turned as even now she turned to the silk-lined oak wall below the vault lid damming the clay above and bonemarrowed sightless sockets below. Had it been another's funeral, how stunning she would have looked, white gloves and white corsage, navy blue dress and hat, and shoes now unseen. Some undertakers sell slacks from suits. Well, they say, they're never seen in the casket anyway. Do they sell skirts too, and shoes?

And down the other wall, pictures of his son, from birth to the last picture, the bearded farmer, now thirty-eight, who lived in a distant town and walked furrows to a different harvest. His wife and son side-slipped past him on the stairs, oscillating the amorphous perimeter of lifedeath. He would go to his son's and take the towed speed of Rosie there.

While hitching up Rosie he looked through the trees and beyond the fields. Rosie turned, nuzzling her head into his. He held her there, looking out to the fields they'd worked in another day heel to toe.

"They would buy the fields and build houses, the real estate people would, if we'd sell. We could be rich," he said in her ear. "But we like the thrust of it, the windsweep space of it, room to pee without rushing to coppered plumbing, to let the weeds grow now, to walk a crooked row." A light whinny came and she stomped her feet in the sod.

"There is a loneliness here some days and I long to see my son," he whispered now, "but there is a greater loneliness then in seeing him … them. It is not what it was when he was home with us, the boyhood jokes and joy of it."

The sloped gravel shoulder of the road was wide and he kept Rosie to the right. A horn sounded from the red, white, and blue jeep. The mailman stopped on the far shoulder and called across. "Rosie looks good this morning, and your buggy." He thumbed into a box of mail. "I have a letter for you, from your son."

"Never mind. Give it to me tomorrow, not even today in the box. I don't want to visit them because of the letter or not visit them because of the letter." He pulled lightly on the reins and Rosie settled. "I will go because I am going and will not stop going until I get there and have gone."

"As you wish, Otto. Have a good trip."

He pulled lightly, flipping the reins on Rosie's rump and sucking a tweet between his pursed lips. He knew many of the drivers who passed and they waved or tooted. One stopped to ask him if he wanted a lift. Otto held up an apple and laughed. Sometimes the shoulder slanted off steeply and when no cars were coming he hawed Rosie from the shoulder. He was lulled into foot-tapping and humming to the rhythmic gait Rosie laid down.

He turned then to see a spruce tree taller than the maples in the field and a dog barked. He knew that he and Rosie could go into the field and rest or even sleep until the night, and then go home in the dark when traffic was lighter, and look in the dark for their farm.

He let the easy rhythm of Rosie relax him and knew the cars passing were dangerously close and did not slow. "I could stand up in my buggy and talk to those drivers, warn them, but they have time only for the place down the road they are headed for."

The tempo was disturbed when Rosie's left front foot caught part of a pothole. She limped out of the gait. Otto saw the cattails come closer as he geed Rosie to the shoulder and whoad her. Her foot and leg showed no visible injury.

They walked slowly to the next sideroad and turned, and turned again into the lane of G. Morley & Sons, so the white paint on red barnwood announced. A collie barked and then wagged his tail and came closer.

"Talk to him, girl, settle him." She had a way with dogs. Otto looked around for someone at the farm and heard a door slam. A farmer approached, bending over now to pet the prancing collie.

"Trouble with your mare?" He put out his hand, leathered and tanned, "I'm George Morley," and he looked up at the sign on the barn as if for confirmation.

"Otto. Rosie caught the corner of a pothole back there. I think she'll be all right with a bit of a rest. She's hit more than that in her time. My fields are stone loaded."

"Unhitch her. I'll have my girls feed and water her, rub her down."

"Your boys," Otto corrected him, looking up at the '& Sons.'

"No boys." He kicked a stone and the collie started for it. "Ever see '& Daughters' on a barn?"

"Once. This would have been twice. Might encourage thrice."

"Would have been, might have been, who knows."

"I was on the way to visit my son."

George was called in to the phone and his daughter came over to Otto. She was the age of Otto's son, wore blue bib overalls and a wide-brimmed straw hat with her hair up under it.

"We haven't had a horse on the farm for twenty years or more," she called back, as she led Rosie to the barn.

Otto sat on a tree stump by the buggy and picked a stem of grass and put it between his teeth. A shadow passed over him. He looked up. "I thought you were ... your father?"

"My father will be out in a minute. I'm Frankie, and that's my sister, Joey." She was a few years younger than her sister, wore a blue cap with a long peak, high work shoes with her pantlegs tucked in. "You have a nice horse."

"Rosie. We were going to my son's."

"How far does your son live?"

"He lives in Maumee, I guess about twenty miles from here."

"Does he visit you often?"

"Maybe twice a year he comes, since he's married. I suppose if you had the tools to do it you could see it in my eyes, or you could measure the floor covering I've worn going to the window to look out for him, or the depth of wrinkles. Days and nights wondering."

She looked at him for a moment, not speaking. Some chickens scattered squawking near the fence. "Do you have chickens on your farm?"

"I got the eggs, or my wife did … then. And when they stopped laying I didn't have the heart to eat them. Might have done them more a favour with the ax than old age. Rosie gets on well with your sister."

"I'm sure Rosie gets on well with everyone."

"Are you sure? How can you be sure? If you had a husband you would be sure of nothing."

She looked at her left hand, her bare ring finger. "We used to have our chickens fenced in." A crow landed in a cottonwood tree, high up, and began to caw-caw. "I don't always know what I think. It helps sometimes to talk to someone."

Otto moved his hand to a low spoke on the buggy wheel. "I haven't had such a conversation with a woman in many years." He looked up at the crow.

"You have such conversations with men?"

"I never expect it, except with my son, and so I count no failures."

She saw her father coming and excused herself. Then, pushing her shadow ahead of her, she walked over to her sister and Rosie. Watching her walk, Otto turned then to see George approach.

"I can decipher Rosie's language, but how many other things ... and people ... are trying to talk to me, over my head? Have you paid your taxes yet?"

Moving into Otto's pain, George was jarred with the question. "I ..."

"Do you put up any strawberries for the winter?" Otto took a large blue handkerchief from his pocket and blew his nose loudly.

"We ..."

"The south wall of your barn does not look level. Your daughters get on well with Rosie."

"They get along with everything and everyone, I believe." He had been squatting haunches to heel and now turned an old bucket over and sat down facing Otto. "If I'd realized that, I'd never had to put 'and Sons' on the redbarnwood or had their blood spilled red in the river." George clenched his right hand into a fist taut and white across the knuckles. "My wife ..."

"You don't have to tell me anything. I'm no chaplain."

"It's all right. My wife had the girls the first year and

28

the third after we were married. The doctor said she wouldn't have any more children. She was happy but I had to have a son, for the farm, for the name. We adopted one and then the other, right around the ages of the girls at the time. They were a problem from the beginning, didn't get along with the girls, with my wife, with me. Everything we did for them was wrong. And they were always fighting each other."

Otto and then George stood up, moved to the back of the buggy, staying in the sun. "One afternoon, they were fifteen by then, they decided, I suppose, to settle all their grudges in one big battle. I still don't know all the details, but I know how it ended. They were always racing each other on the horses, yes, the last two horses we had on this farm. But a race wasn't good enough for that grudge. They took pitchforks from the barn, and went at it over on the back forty and in the river, where it ended. McCurdy my neighbour first saw them when he was plowing his land beside mine there. He shouted but nothing and no one was going to stop them by then. Jeff speared Mike's horse and as the horse was buckling under, he speared Mike too. They both fell in the river, Mike and his horse. It wasn't deep there, and there was blood for some time, the bank and high spots on rocks."

"The day I lost my son," Otto started.

"Wait," George snapped and put his hands out as if to silence the whole countryside. Otto looked around, waiting for someone to come, something to be heard in the silence. In a few minutes George said, very softly, "I am always struck by how soon we want to tell something else when death's body is still warm. Life going on. I think we need a period of mourning, of silence."

Chastened as someone who might have said the same thing, fought the same space where sadness and anger contend, Otto looked up to an old kite remnant caught on high branches of an elm. "You are right. I'm sorry." And he looked down. "It has passed. I have not forgotten what I was going to say nor why I wanted to say it just then. It will keep." A tractor passed along the road, and it was quiet again.

Otto and George looked over to the barn where the daughters were taping Rosie's leg.

"If you wish, you could leave Rosie here and go on to your son's. We could drive you down the road to catch the bus."

"It is not clear now what I will do, Rosie there, the buggy here. As the crow flies," and he looked up.

"Feel free to stay overnight at your son's, if you wish. Rosie will be fine here. Really, I don't know how you are going to take her away when you come back, my girls love her so."

Otto felt a strange and sudden coldness in his legs and a light shiver rolled up his body. Rosie would be all right, the son would be all right, and the fields and barn and house at the farm. Perhaps it was time.

"I will go on to see my daughter, and your sons will take care of my elephant."

"Strange, I almost corrected you," George said, kicking a stone beside the buggy wheel. "Well, I have to be going to the mill. I can give you a lift to the bus route. You are welcome to stay or come along."

"Rosie is settled down with your daughters. I will not say good-bye to her."

Otto got out of George's car at the highway. "You can catch the bus right on that corner across the road." Otto watched George pull away and then stop on the shoulder about a quarter mile down the road. Otto turned in time to flag down the bus. He sat on the right side so he could see George in passing. George was waving frantically, standing outside his car.

"Your friend seems upset about something," a man said, sitting in front of Otto, looking back at George still waving.

"He's keeping my horse."

"My Ralphie wants a horse," a woman sitting across the aisle said, turning to Otto. "Maybe you can take some of that nonsense out of his head. You know, how much bother they are, the expense of food and all that, and how dangerous it is riding them ..."

"Rosie doesn't eat much. I had an aquarium once cost more. Got it for Christmas. Never would've bought it myself."

The man turned again. "There goes your friend passing the bus, that's him on the horn." George drove to the next crossroad and jumped out of his car to flag down the bus.

"Sorry to stop you, I don't want to get on, but ..."

"What is this, mister, either get on or get off. I've got a schedule to make."

"There's a man on here going in the wrong direction. He should be on the ... Oh, Otto, you need the southbound bus, the other direction."

"Will you still take care of Rosie if I go this way for a while yet?"

"We'll take care of Rosie. It's you I'm worried about." The bus driver sounded the horn and flipped the switch on and off to close the door. George got off and the bus jerked away.

"See the trouble, Ralphie, all because of a horse."

Two men behind Otto were talking about muscle cars, horsepower two hundred and more. Otto went to the back of the bus to stretch out on the long empty seat across the back, and went to sleep. He and Rosie were waiting patiently on a sideroad for the highway traffic to clear so they could cross. Traffic was snout and muzzle to bumper, each car pulled by two hundred horses. Otto bent over to pick some grass for Rosie and when he straightened up his shoulder bumped into something, and he woke up to the bus driver poking him on the shoulder.

"You can't sleep on this bus, mister. I think that guy was right, you're going in the wrong direction." The bus driver cursed as he walked back to his seat, and again jerked the bus as it started up.

"He was rude to wake you up. There are plenty of seats," a man said from a nearby seat by the window.

"But no beds."

"Just as well you can make light of it."

"Let there be light," Otto said as he stood up. "I only stand because it is nice riding the bus this way, not because of what I heard and not because I am ready to get off. It is really a joke. My tooth hurts or I would laugh."

"I think you have a nice smile when you laugh," the man said.

"My father and a teacher called it a smirk and slapped my face. Do you have a compass?" Otto asked. "My father would recognize me with my smirk. He would not have to call me or smell me or see my ID."

The man moved back to sit across from Otto, putting his bag down beside Otto's bag, and in a few minutes he took Otto's bag and rang the bell to get off the bus.

"Maybe I should keep quiet," Otto said loudly. "You may have more than apples and bread in your bag."

The man came back and snatched the bag away from Otto and dropped the other bag on Otto's feet. "Sorry," and he turned and got off the bus.

Otto jumped up and followed off. The man waved his hand high in the air without turning around to Otto, and walked down the road. Otto crossed the road and stumbled where the height of the towering ironweed deceived him at the ditchfall. In the chickory-spread field he found a maple and fit the smooth bark into his back and dozed off for half an hour.

When he awoke he looked for his bag, to have an apple. "You must have been here all the time," he said, when he found it beside his left thigh. "Surely you're not playing tricks on me." Some slate-coloured juncos lighted on the ground nearby and he pulled a slice of bread from his bag and tore off bits to throw to them, but they were startled by his arm swing and flew away. Soon jagged lines of ants trooped up and swarmed over the bread.

He began walking along the road shoulder, to the south this time, turning down sideroads, off into bird-flocked fields, exploring mud-washed ravines and river banks. At nightfall he saw an open fire beyond a treeclump bordering a river. Two men, unshaven and sitting against white birch, watched him approach.

"Got an extra bunk?" Otto asked.

"If you can pay the tariff," the short one said, shifting from the tree to lean on his other elbow.

"Sit down, sit down," the tall man said. "Don't mind him." But in the night by the light of the fire, Otto could see it was the tall one who looked through his bag and then lay down again.

At daybreak a scout troop of eight boys and their leader marched single-file past the fire, turned and continued to the north. Each of them had a compass in hand and a flashlight. A half hour or so later they had reversed directions and passed near the fire again. Although it was daylight now, each boy still shined his flashlight, veering off momentarily in answer to his own compass call and then falling back in line.

Otto left his bag by the still-sleeping tall man's feet and walked back to the road. He went on to a store and asked the time for the next southbound bus, then had a cup of coffee and a roll and got on the bus half an hour later.

After a thirty-minute ride he was at his son's road. He walked west for twenty minutes or so and then walked back. There were flowers and fine spruce and birch trees and a birdhouse in the front yard at his son's. A cardinal, feeding in the scarlet-berried yew, flew to the top of the birch.

Otto went to the door and reached out for the

doorbell. He withdrew his hand and held it midair. He heard Sparky bark a few times, in the basement probably, and he waited. It was quiet and he turned and walked away.

Flight 210

SHE WANTED to say it and say all of it, the satin bed-sheets and bloodstain of it, the Tom Collinses and thick-ness in the throat, and he would not hear it. In the end, none of it would make any difference, what he knew; but in the beginning he wanted to stay clear and clean of it.

"First it was in Chicago," she would start. "We were on our way to …"

"It's all right," he would interrupt as one interrupts a child who has skinned his knee and sobs beyond the range of the pain. He would stop her lips moving and kiss the words back in and hold her until she stopped shaking.

"You should listen. Let me tell it; then there was Toronto."

"*You* listen. You're my wife and that's all that matters now."

They would be close then and when it was over she would cry.

"So beautiful, gentle," and when she tried to say more, he sensed the danger in it and filled the time with talk. His mother used to tell him things as he backed against the wall, too young to understand what she was saying, when he had to listen. Only years later did it make any sense, and it was too late then not to hear it. Although she talked of events of the past, he felt he was an unwilling accomplice to evil yet to happen, and he churned inwardly to ward it off.

His wife had thought she could pursue him recklessly, that his good judgment would save them from each other at the last moment, that he would never marry her. Now it seemed like some worrisome flaw in him that he had bought the ring and said the vows. At first she felt deceived. How could he do that to her, and how could he set himself adrift so effortlessly?

Then through slow and painful increments she reconstructed the pursuit and how she came to be a different person: she moved from alcohol to malted milks with him, walks in the country replaced dancing, she gave up friends to be alone with him.

There seemed nothing sacrificial about the changes at the time; she knew she had not intended anything permanent. Now, in telling him things of her past, she wanted him to see what a mistake they had made, even he had made, so that he would let her go, and she could shed her guilt and be once more all her guilt was made for.

There were doubts before they married, but one by one he had answered them, not with certainties but with possibilities. He had buried his doubts and would not let them surface again. No old closet skeletons would be exhumed.

She gave up trying to say it, to match words with her urgent inner whispers and screams. She sought not release from conflict and punishment but exciting passage through them. She needed a stronger language than words, one that only flailing arms and teetering walk could articulate. She began drinking heavily. It would tell him what her words had failed to say.

It started at parties. The office held one or two a month, and she drank more at each one than at the last. She was furious when he did not fight or blame her. She was trying to make a conspicuous protest and she wanted a conspicuous and vehement response. But he treated her delicately, as if she were ill and needed help with her unsteadiness, quietly wakened her if she slept it off in the hostess's bedroom, or cleaned her up if she vomited.

She expanded her area of protest and began drinking at home. He would come home from work and see the car angled across the driveway toward the lawn, the door still open, and car radio blaring through the trees and down the block. The inside of the house resembled the scene of a minor explosion after the dust and flying objects have settled and the stillness is at odds with all of the visual clues. Broom and mop lay where some unsteady grasp had released them, pots were tilted off the stove or tumbled out of cupboards. Bottles at various levels of emptiness were hidden in closets and behind curtains and in the washer and dryer and oven.

At first she drank vodka. "It'll leave me breathless," she slurred. Like choosing a lion for a house pet, he thought, because its soft-padded feet would be noiseless across the kitchen floor.

When he came in after work those days, she would be sprawled on the sofa. She rebuffed his attempts to replace the soiled pillow or wipe her face or put a cover on her. He would clean up the house and fix dinner, but she seldom ate until the next day. He didn't eat but sat down with Jimmy, her seven year old son from her first marriage.

Later she would talk. "I've got to get out of here. Let me go. Kick me out," she muddled, raising her arm to halt him when he tried to approach her. She looked up at the ceiling as if needing the aid of some cue cards posted there, to say it right, so he would agree. He waited. In a few minutes she softened her tone. "You've been good to Jimmy and ... but life is more than that, than this," and she threw her arms open, surveying the wreckage.

"I'm sorry."

"Sorry? Why be sorry? Be glad we found it out now. Why wait till all the ends are frayed, all the ugly things said. You're trying desperately to save it and I'm trying to scrap it. Why not now?" The vodka helped her say it and the saying sobered her.

"There must have been something in the first place or why did we get married?" He moved toward the sofa, to sit on the edge beside her, but she flopped over and took up the space.

"Lust probably, legitimizing the jumping into bed."

He flinched at that. "You're forgetting what brought us together in the first place. Afraid maybe of looking foolish now." He checked himself from reminding her how she gave up drinking before they were married or from reminding himself how naively he thought it would be permanent.

"If you'd just let me leave, you wouldn't have to go through all this crap," and she slurred again.

"But why would I let you go? I love you."

"Why?"

"You're my wife."

"That doesn't make me lovable. I'm different now. Or haven't you noticed ..." and on a hiccup and lowered octave she added, "... the transformation?"

"You're still ..."

"Have you taken a good look lately?" she interrupted, shaking her head to throw the hair over her face.

"You're still the one I married," and he reached over to put her hair back, but she pulled away, turning her head.

"Then you're either stupid or so damn nice you won't see it." She pushed herself up on one elbow. "You're an old string saver. You never get rid of anything. And now you won't let *me* go."

It was true. She had to throw out his old shoes and shirts when he was not home. If he saw them in the trash, he retrieved them as old friends. Frequently asked when he was going to put his old dog to sleep, he quipped, "Oh, Duke doesn't need any help sleeping. He naps on and off all day and still sleeps all night." His wide and narrow lapel suits went into and out of storage, by turn, as they went in and out of fashion.

And when the lot next door was sold and he saw the bulldozer come in to level it, he scooped the polliwogs from the low spots into a bucket and dug a hole in his own yard for them. Then he transplanted the wild strawberry plants to a border near his own garden.

One Saturday afternoon they went to an auction in the country, and she pointed out a man who kept making smart remarks, interrupting the auctioneer. "That was Jimmy's father at the auction," she said on the way home. "I'm glad Jimmy wasn't with us today."

He was shocked. "How could you live with someone like that? And marry him?"

"How can you?"

"You're not like that."

"Neither was he ... all the time. He was real good most of the time, and that helped me through the rough times. And then some strange sort of balance shifted and he got mean, just like I'm getting. Maybe you'll see now why I wish you'd hate me, throw me out, stop trying to be so damn nice to me."

Thinking what her first marriage must have been like, it was not only easier for him to be "nice" to her; it was compelling. Sometimes he would get up at night and walk through the house and wish it was always that quiet and peaceful. He would tidy it then and it was clean. Once at 3 AM he was mopping and turned to see her watching him. He went over to hug her and she slapped his face and then tore up the room. He never tried that again.

"Why don't you fight back, knock me around? Everyone changes after marriage. What's wrong with you? Everyone finds their own level of meanness after the honeymoon. What do you hold on for? Hit me and I can feel good about leaving."

For a moment, a brief and scary moment, he felt like smashing the dirty dishes in the kitchen and tearing the curtains from the windows, and saying, "This isn't where the ketchup belongs, it should be screaming through big smears and streaks on the white walls." But the urge passed quickly, and he went trembling to the basement and walked around and around until he stopped panting and shaking and sweating and he felt the chill of the concrete floor on his bare feet. The floor above him creaked and he heard her walk to another room and slowly he climbed the stairs.

He felt he was holding on, to whatever it was, as he might hold on to flimsy and brittle branches in climbing a hill, and that any moment they could snap in two or pull out of the ground and he would lurch backwards.

He was schooled for such a marriage and would keep trying to make it work. His parents had endured a joyless marriage and his sister was still in one. He thought one reason he had married was to rescue her and Jimmy, identifying them with his mother and himself. He remembered how it was in his childhood when his father left them for weeks at a time. He had wanted to take his mother away to a home where it would be quiet and no one would leave. And now, although they lived together, they each lived a different marriage: she her first marriage and he his parents' marriage.

She got pregnant and he thought she would forget about leaving. But when Toddy was born, she drank more, and he cared for the baby much of the time.

He held him in the rocking chair, lifting a corner of the blanket, gently touching the bump on the back of the baby's head. She had been drinking when she dropped him from the bed.

The swelling was going down. He brushed his lips softly across the golden hairs and down the smooth warm neck and then rolled the blanket back.

He hummed low with the rhythmic creak of the pressed floor, his heels up and down with each arc of the rocker. He turned his face into a fold in the blanket, like a duck with its bill feathered back into its side for warmth.

Sounds of stumbling from the front steps jolted him to a tight hold on the baby and he got up. He walked quickly in the dark across the slanting floor to the kitchen, through the doorway slightly narrowed by bookcases on each side, now holding pots and pans.

He heard the storm door open and the key crisscross the inner door and knob and lockplate before it hit the keyhole and turned. The door banged open against the darkened floor lamp and then slammed shut.

He went out the back door to the utility room, locking the door lightly, and sat down on the woodpile. The baby turned but continued sleeping. He heard her retching in the bathroom and the toilet flushing, and it was quiet again.

Near the end of the woodpile three maple logs, cradled by smaller branches, formed a place where he'd sat before, for times like this, and gently he rocked the baby again. In time he opened the door slowly, turned off the light, and from practice found his way in the dark to the crib. He covered the baby and knelt beside the crib, shivering, his arms and chest cold from the warmth withdrawn.

He lay down on the rug beside the crib, rolling in a blanket and pulling the rug like a pocket flap over himself. It was a long time before he didn't smell vomit anymore. He slept until the lightest turn in the crib woke him instantly, and it was quiet again and they slept.

When she talked of leaving, she talked of taking Toddy as well as Jimmy. The prospect terrified him. He feared for Toddy's safety and his own sanity if Toddy were taken away. But he had to be careful how he expressed his concern to her.

He would stay and hold on, not risk losing Toddy by leaving or letting her go. Anything was better than losing Toddy. When she talked of leaving he would have some prospect to put a stake in the future: "We'll get our seed catalog in March. We'll buy a pear tree next spring and then we'll have to wait and see it bloom. We'll plant perennials, not annuals," and she stayed.

"You don't have to hide bottles anymore either." They would buy the beer and wine together and drink it together. No hiding, no rush to empty bottles. They bought it together. She drank it alone. She bought other bottles and hid them again.

"Why don't you hit me, why don't you hate me and let me go?" she goaded him.

"I guess I feel responsible in some way for your drinking, so I want to help work it out."

"Oh, dear God, deliver me," and she rolled her eyes. "The more you hold on the worse it gets. It's like all your virtues are vices to me. Goodie goodie patience and forgiveness are so damned divine, they infuriate me!"

He would try to calm her and realize she didn't want to be calmed. She sought an excitement that was not with him, he thought, but probably more in the disturbances of her first marriage. She seemed determined – or was it resigned – to go on or back to something like that, where she could feel alive again in the exciting turmoil and seductive pain of it. And what, exciting and seductive or somehow rewarding, was there in it for him as well, the willing or hesitant accomplice?

Frequently he had to clean the kitchen sink before preparing a meal or washing the dishes, and he often had to clean the vomit from the bathroom sink or bathtub before he could get the boys ready for bed.

He sat by Toddy's youth bed at bedtime and made up stories about Sammy the raccoon. There were two pic-

45

tures of raccoons on the wall beside Toddy's bed: one cut from a magazine and one that Toddy had drawn with crayons, a brown body hanging from a green tree, and two yellow eyes peeking out from behind a smiling black mask.

It was a different story each night: one night Sammy went to the ice cream store looking for licorice ice cream to match his mask; another night he visited the library looking for a picture of a little boy, but he checked out a Polaroid camera instead and took a picture of Toddy to tack up on the wall of his tree house, inside the hole he keeps peeking out of. When Toddy laughed and was excited, his father toned down the story for a quiet ending, and time for sleep.

One night, he tucked the blanket around Toddy, who turned and was soon asleep. Jimmy was still awake on the other side of the room, and asked, "Do people kill raccoons?"

"Sometimes hunters do."

Jimmy struggled with quivering lips. "I killed a deer," and his voice broke to a whimper. His father had taken him on a hunting trip with another man two years earlier. "My father shot a deer. It was down by a tree when we got there, bleeding a lot in the neck. It wasn't dead yet and my father put me inside his arms and behind the gun and told me to pull the trigger." It took Jimmy a minute to find his voice again.

"The deer kept looking at me, and there was blood, and my father put his hand over mine and pulled the trigger." His father and the other man slapped Jimmy's back and called him "killer" and laughed. The deer did not move then but its eyes still looked up at Jimmy.

Toddy was his own child but Jimmy pulled him too. They had sailed many kites together, thrown baseballs and footballs and played marbles. Yet he knew Jimmy would go away when she went and Jimmy knew it too, and they both kept some distance to deal with that day and that separation.

When he had first come in the room to put Toddy and Jimmy to bed, the light was still coming in the window, so it might have been difficult to tell, had one not known, if it was morning or evening. Only by waiting would one know if the light brightened into the dawn or darkened deeper, throwing shadows and dreams ahead. Now the light had faded from the room, receding to the outdoors where it evaporated into the night.

One evening he found her sitting on the sidewalk in front of a store, sitting beside a one-legged man who had his cap on the walk and some pencils angled out of the cap and coins in it. The man was playing an accordion and she was singing, "My Wild Irish Rose," although he was playing "Star Dust." She sang louder, and hollered at him when he tried to get her to go home with him. He went to the car and waited where he could see her until the stores closed and she staggered up and the accordion player left.

They had been staying together for the sake of the children, he thought, but he knew he would never separate until she agreed to his custody of Toddy. He could not push that too much or she would just take Toddy and leave.

The propeller was from an old fan stored in the attic. It could be used now for something important. Toddy was two and a half and he had been talking to Toddy about the airplane and gathering supplies. He thought of the kildeer, so skillful at distracting those who came near its nest, and he thought of the plane again that he and Toddy would build.

She needed to leave in her own way, her own time. She would not leave if he pleaded for her to stay, and she backed off from leaving when he finally seemed agreeable to it. And when he said nothing she reacted to *that*. It was more than he that held her there.

Then he got sick: headaches, high fever, sleeplessness, and the skin on his thighs sensitive as if he'd been sunburned, but no marks on it. He was hospitalized for tests. It was polio. He worried at the hospital, wondering what was happening at home, with her drinking. One time she had let the water run over the kitchen sink and flood the floors. Another time the pans burned dry on the stove and almost caused a fire, filling the house with smoke.

There was time to think then, to think about dying and new ways of living if you recover, and what changes you'll make before the old ways turn you into a corpse.

She said it every time she came to the hospital for visiting hours, said what he had been thinking but was afraid to say for fear she would fight it or fear she would accept it: nothing would get better until they separated.

What is this carrying on one dizzying mistake after another, he thought, carrying it down to the second and third generations. Like the colour of eyes and shape of fingers, the moon of fingernails, and the walk, and now again and again failure in marriage and the grim endurance of it, so that it is the other one, the spouse, who leaves. Looking at Toddy he wondered what he had given him that he too would be caught in a web unable to escape. Something he'd inherited or picked up as simply as he picked up the way to pronounce words or to eat spaghetti or to walk.

He worked hard at the hospital with the leg brace and crutches for his polio, and finally was discharged.

He and Toddy went to the farmers' market one morning. They had separate bags of lettuce and oranges, celery and potatoes, and they were looking for a box to keep them all together. They saw a wooden apple box. The man didn't want to let it go, but when they told him they were going to use it in Toddy's airplane, he sold it to them for half a dollar.

"Do you mind if we write down some things, sort of an agreement?" he had said one night when they were sitting quietly before going to bed. "You've wanted to go for years. If it does happen, someday, I hope we can do it without any battles and courts and all that. I just thought if we could put some things down on paper maybe it would help. Instead of leaving it all to the lawyers."

She hesitated. "All right," but he sensed she was moving away from it even as she agreed.

He waited, not wanting to cause more reaction, and

in a few weeks he wrote down some points, a rough draft, to talk over with her. She had to agree or it would not work. If they couldn't agree he would stick it out. It wasn't property he was concerned about, but always having Toddy. He would give up everything else to have custody of Toddy, and by custody he meant sole custody.

He thought of Solomon's judgment, struggling to call on a higher authority to support him in what he knew most people would oppose. Many children would do better with one parent than split up, back and forth, *you the weekend and I the week, you for Christmas and I Thanksgiving. And how do we divide the summer down the middle? Will it ever be fair if you take him to the zoo and movies and I remind him of homework and scraping the mud off his feet, take him to the dentist for drilling and to the doctor for shots?*

He shuddered to think of Toddy going with her and having to live with a father like Jimmy's or riding in her car as it crashed into trees and ran into ditches.

He didn't write all of it down but he talked about it. He was generous with the property because Toddy was all he wanted. She had nothing to add to the paper. She said nothing, and he wondered if she would agree now just to be gone, and later fight it when she'd thought about it.

They found a long nail to mount the propeller on the end of the apple crate, using washers so it would spin freely. "But we call it the 'fuselage' now, not the apple crate. Now, what's next? The wings!"

Two months past Toddy's third birthday she said she would leave. The moving van came early that Saturday morning, and she and Jimmy packed the car with small things.

They took the apple crate from the garage and put it back in the yard under the big oak tree, on the picnic table there, next to the swing. They'd set aside a piece of plywood for the wings and nailed it under the apple crate so the overhang was about even on each side. They put the supplies they would need for the plane in the garage so they didn't have to go in the house while she was packing and moving things out to her car down the driveway.

Toddy found wheels and knobs from tinker toy and erector sets and together they wrote numbers around the knobs to represent air speed and altitude, and fastened them to the inside behind the propeller. An old steering wheel from a toy car was then mounted and steadied with wire. A small cushion was Toddy's seat, and he climbed in to check out his instruments.

She was at the corner of the house by the yard. "I'm going to gas up. I'll be back," and she didn't wait for an answer.

"I'll get the pilot some milk and cookies," he said to Toddy, "before you take off on Flight 210."

He went into the house and looked at the rooms now larger with some furniture removed. In the living room his rocker and a magazine rack were at opposite ends of the room, but he filled in the sofa between them and saw her lying on it.

All the rotten times were gone now and he thought of the good times they'd had: Toddy's birth, picnics and vacation trips and birthday parties.

He took the cookies and milk outside and hooked up the ropes from the swing to the apple crate and added another rope to steady it at the back. Toddy finished his snack and then she was back and had been drinking. He could always tell, that look in her eyes. Jimmy stood at the corner of the house and she came into the yard.

She stood there and smiled at Toddy. He moved the dials and the steering wheel and made louder and louder noises for his plane. She hugged Toddy and told him to have a good plane ride. And then, struggling to hold back the tears, she turned and waved and walked ten feet or so. He followed her and she turned around.

"Take care of yourself, Channy."

"I was going to turn around to see who you were talking to, it's been so long since you've called me by name."

"I know you'll take care of Toddy," and they touched hands. Toddy revved the plane to a higher pitch.

"Marla," and it was as if they were being introduced. "There is so much more to say. That all the years and what we've been through could end like this …"

"Don't," she said, turning away, and they squeezed hands slightly and she walked away. Jimmy had been leaning against the corner of the house, and as he pushed himself away to go with her, his hand gave the slightest wave.

He said "yes" and "oh, good," and "fine" automatically and mechanically to Toddy for the next several minutes, listening for the car to start and pull away. Then he turned from the street to the back yard. It looked like Flight 210 would leave this time. It had been scheduled and cancelled and rescheduled many times but it looked like it would finally leave. It would leave in an apple crate with tinker toy fittings and a propeller from an old unrepaired attic fan, all things saved for just such a day.

He gave Toddy another push and walked to the back fence. Two boys were cutting across the school yard corner in the long grass and a kildeer called out, flapping near the ground to distract them. "There must be a nest there," he said into the wind and it blew past him and threw Toddy's long hair back.

"Will we get a green car too?" Toddy asked, his plane slowing down until he got another push.

"Green or blue, red, white, silver, oh yes, Toddy, there are lots of colors."

"And will we plant the pear tree too?"

Birthday Wish

HE HAD WANTED to get it straight and remember it truly from the beginning. He doubted if he would be able to recall the details of the ordeal he and his son were going through if he did not write it down as it happened. There would be days in the hospital, later, when he could not write, but he did not know that at the beginning.

Sat., Aug. 23 – Marla phoned. Chev battery dead at 7 Mile Road. Went for her. Pushed car and got new battery. She was drunk, had left car radio playing, ran battery down. Later at home she vomited on the bed. House a shambles. Todd not feeling well. Cleaned vomit from sinks so I could get him washed and to bed.

Sun., Aug. 24 – Up several times with Todd during the night, for water, fruit juice. He was feverish. Marla up a number of times vomiting. Sinks and bath tub full of vomit again. Todd running 101 fever. His tonsils swollen. Worried about polio. Phoned doctor and got aspirin substitute and flavored penicillin tablets.

Mon., Aug. 25 – Todd feeling his old self again. Moving furniture so I can get to the interior trim and baseboard. Very tense and feeling pushed with all the jobs lined up to do.

Fri., Sept. 5 – My thighs very sore, the skin itself tender, just like a sunburn. No marks on legs. Probably from bending over working on baseboard and up and down ladder to work on trim and paint. Took aspirin but no change. Got four more rooms ready and stained the trim.

Sat., Sept. 6 – Walking downtown and my legs very sore when we got home. Also headache and pain in back and arms.

Sun., Sept. 7 – Hardly slept a wink last night. Terrific pains in lower back, hips, and thighs. Phoned doctor. He said to take aspirins and use heat; the pain is probably lumbago, he said.

Mon., Sept. 8 – Hardly any pain this morning but my left knee weak and buckles on me. No strength in left leg.

Tues., Sept. 9 – I have to throw both legs stiff-legged when I walk to the bathroom. I had been relying on right leg to hold me up, but it gave way too. Fell down in bathroom when both knees buckled. Still taking aureomycin pills every six hours.

Thurs., Sept. 11 – Phoned Dr. Paness to tell him more of my symptoms: my neck is sore and stiff. The muscles and nerves twitch and jump all over my body. Occasional pains all over. Fever fluctuates around 100. Had been 103.

Fri., Sept. 12 – Dr. Paness over in morning to examine me. Sent me to Herman Kiefer Hospital for spinal tap test for polio. Marla drove, Mother and Todd along too. Test and they sent my clothes home and sent me to Pavilion 6, Room 218, with polio. Ate my supper lying down. Three of us in small room. Couldn't urinate to give them sample. Hardly slept a wink all night. Hal in bed beside me calling for nurse every few minutes.

Mon., Sept. 15 – Started hot packs – Sister Kenny method – on my thighs, back, and neck. Doctor checked me and found my right shoulder has weakened since yesterday.

Fri., Sept. 26 – Dr. Blodgett, the consulting orthopedist, came into room today to check the two room buddies for braces. I was too new to be checked, but I made a supreme bid by sitting up in bed and calling him by name. He came over and was so impressed by my progress that he ordered a full left leg brace for me.

Wed., Oct. 1 – I was out of bed and up in wheel chair for visiting hours and Mother didn't see me. She saw my empty bed and started to cry.

Fri., Oct. 3 – Walking with walker but my right knee started to buckle a little, so didn't go far. Walker was wobbly and I had no shoulder support. Physiotherapist Miss Beck asked me to touch my toes. When I did, she had me "promoted" to the third floor room 318 where I was taken off hot packs.

Tues., Oct. 7 – I stood up and lifted both legs. The therapist said I am the ideal patient. I have the will to get well. I want to get well and go home. I am worried about Todd being home with Marla who is drinking so much.

Wed., Oct. 8 – Marla and Mother late. Marla had been drinking. After they left I put in a plea to go to Pavilion 7 so I could at least go home week-ends.

Thurs., Oct. 9 – Put in another plea to doctor and nurse: "I can whip pain and polio, but I wish I could get home week-ends to help my wife and son." They transferred me to Pavilion 7 and I stood and walked between parallel bars.

Fri., Oct. 10 – Had bath in swirling water of Hubbard tank. Hospital unable to reach Marla by phone to take me home for the weekend, but they got Mother, and she and my brother Walt took me to Mother's as Marla had gone to Battle Creek to her Mother's. Mother phoned her.

Sat., Oct. 11 – Mother and Walt rented wheel chair for me to use at home. Marla back in afternoon with Todd and Jimmy.

Wed., Oct. 15 – Working out on crutches at every opportunity. Got my brace!

Sun., Oct. 19 - Told Marla I am no longer worried about me, my health, polio, but about us.

Discharged me, and I am to take physiotherapy treatments at home. Found the house an obstacle course when I got home, such a mess and Marla drinking.

Mon., Oct. 27 – Poor sleep as I kept thinking of little Todd sobbing to me that Jimmy pushed his nose in soap powder and told him to smell it. Also, has been chasing Todd around the house making horror faces and making him choke when drinking, and touching his penis. Marla slept through it all with her bottles.

Wed., Oct. 29 – Todd and I cut eyes and nose and mouth in his Halloween pumpkin.

Fri., Nov. 1 – Vomit all over the house, on the floor and bedclothes, on dirty dishes in the sink, on her hair.

Mon., Nov. 4 – Missed my physio treatment as Marla had hangover from drinking. Talked with Marla, saying it was getting too much for all of us, that I would agree to a separation now, provided there was no split custody. I am to have sole custody of Todd.

Sat., Dec. 6 – Todd playing doctor and I was his patient. He would like to cure me.

And so eventually the father returned to his work and his studies at the university, wearing a full leg brace, gradually tapering off from two crutches to one, and then to a cane, and then just the brace.

"Will you be able to ride a bicycle some day?" Todd asked his father one afternoon when they were repairing a tire on Grandma's bicycle.

"Oh, I sure think I will. Don't you?"

"Yes. Grandma got this bike from you, didn't she? But she wished for it when she was little like me."

"I see you two have been talking. Yes, I was able to help Grandma's wish come true. And after forty years, think of that. Never give up on wishes. I might even be able to ride Grandma's bike some day."

"Yes," Todd said, happy with the idea, "I think Grandma's bike is magic."

That evening they were lying on the grass, studying dandelions. It was serious business, you could tell. And then Todd's head cradled softly in the fold of his father's elbow, and his father looked through the boy's light brown hair into the setting sun.

They found and picked the "goldenest" dandelions and then held them under each other's chin to see if they liked butter.

Even when the father hadn't shaved for a day or two, his son looked closely and always found the gold of butter between the whiskers. The boy brushed harder then with the dandelions and the gold came off onto the whiskers. "You have gold hair, gold whiskers now," he laughed, "and you like butter." The boy rolled on his back and kicked his legs into the air.

"Your hair is golden all the time," the father said, running his hand through it and over it.

The boy brushed the dandelion under his own chin and said it tickled him and he laughed and shivered at the tickling.

The father moved his son's head gently and started to get up clumsily. Because of his leg brace he had to roll over on his hands and knees and push himself up and then lock the brace at the knee again.

At times he walked without his brace, it was so heavy and awkward. Sometimes then his weak leg buckled under him and he fell, and after bad falls he was on crutches again. The boy came closer then, after the falls, walking beside his father, his hand always ready to try and prevent another fall.

And when the boy was alone he played with a puppet, releasing the strings to let the puppet start to fall, but raising the string just before the puppet hit the floor. Doing this over and over, each time pulling the puppet up a little sooner, so that eventually it just tripped slightly but did not fall.

The boy glued little pieces of sandpaper on the puppet's shoes so it would not slip, and when the snow and ice came, he glued larger pieces of sandpaper on his father's shoes.

Now as the father started to get up, the boy reached over to touch him, to come back down on the grass. They both turned on their backs, and the boy's head found a pillow again in the fold of his father's elbow.

When the sun set the sky began to darken, but the grass was warm and they continued to lie there. "When will the first star be out?" the boy asked.

"Oh, we'll just have to keep looking." And the father remembered the rhyme from his mother, the boy's grandmother. He touched the boy's hair as he said it softly and looked up to the sky.

> *Star light, star bright,*
> *First star I see tonight.*
> *I wish I may, I wish I might*
> *Have the wish I wish tonight.*

As he recited the rhyme, the father saw the boy move his own lips to say it; then he quickly turned and put his fingers over his father's lips. "Shhh," he whispered, "don't tell it or it won't come true."

"You can wish too, then," and the father touched his

son's head and wondered what secret wishes were cradled there.

"I do, I do," and the boy turned his head to see other parts of the darkening sky, "but I won't tell." The father thought one night he'd dream it clear. He'd wish for himself on that first star, and waken to know his son's secret, to have it released to his care as the one who could best fill the boy's wish.

After putting his son to bed, the father sat alone on the grass. Except for the stars, the night was dark. Except for the crickets singing, the night was silent. And then from the other side of the thick hedge a voice came softly and he struggled to get up to hear it better.

He walked around the hedge and toward his son's room. The boy was asleep in bed, as he had left him.

On their birthdays they made silent wishes before blowing out their birthday candles. They often received as gifts many of the things they wished for because earlier in the year they had talked about such things and even dropped hints along the way.

After the polio, the father thought the boy was making fewer wishes and some with no clues or hints to help the father guess. The boy was delighted with whatever gifts he got, but there seemed to the father a distant look in his son's eyes as if a secret wish went unfilled. The father talked to the boy's grandmother about it.

"I know some things about another boy. He never put into spoken words the secret wish he wanted most. This particular little boy is the same. He does more than wish: he worked with a puppet to keep it from falling, and he walked close to his daddy to keep him from falling. And he put sandpaper on the soles of the puppet's and his father's shoes. He made a lot of wishes on stars and at wishing wells, and with wish bones and in prayers, and before blowing out birthday cake candles, but they were never out loud. And, oh, one more thing, if you happen to be talking to him about bikes or toys or wishes or stars, remember it's all very very secret. It's not what he says out loud but what he does that holds the secret."

Long Lake

THEY MADE UP a game at the lake and played it all through the summers Todd was three and four.

On the days they didn't wear bathing suits, they rolled up their pant legs and put their shoes and socks in the old green wooden canvas-covered rowboat. Then they said, "Might as well get in."

Being the oldest, the father pulled rank and sat in the middle seat rowing. Todd sat perched on the small triangular seat in the front. The father would row the boat about a hundred feet out into the lake, calling out, as he slowed or turned, the various ports and islands they passed: "Next stop, Lily Pad Land!" "All aboard for Seaweed City!" "On the starboard side, Black Bass Pond!" "That wonderful vacationland, Bull Frog Island!"

Sometimes Todd wanted to get off at one port or another, and the father would steady him to dip one foot into the water, over the side of the boat, and then pull it back again.

They would laugh when he talked to King Bull Frog or Prince Perch or others on these stop-overs. "Mr. Frog, is all of that your long tail? Or is it just a stem from the lily pad?"

Then they would row back to shore, the long boat trip completed. Todd would say, "Might as well get out," and climb over the side of the boat into the shallow water and wade up to the sand. In a few minutes, after seeing what shore birds were feeding there and checking his crop of cattails, he would say, "Might as well get in," and return to the boat for another ride.

In time Todd came to the middle seat and the two rowed together, each working a separate oar, and laughing as they tried to figure out why the boat went round and round in circles.

And, looking over the side of the boat, they laughed at faces making faces from the water. The ripples twisted their noses longer or shorter and wrinkled ears and mouths. "Look, Daddy, how my arm and hand bend under water. It doesn't hurt at all. Just looks funny." And he dipped his left hand underwater to touch his right hand.

Often they splashed water up onto their faces to cool off from the rowing. And then water dripped from their hands down onto the faces in the water, waterdrops making more ripples there.

Sometimes, when there was a gentle breeze and waves that rocked the boat, they would lie down sideways on the seats or on the floor and have a peaceful rolling nap.

"Daddy, this boat is like a rocking horse," Todd said on days of rolling waves.

They played this game over and over, father and son, never tiring of more rowing and laughing, of getting in and getting out, of one more time.

Years later someone said that the lake had changed, the old green canvas boat had finally been buried by rolling waves of sand, many cottages had been built around the shore, and one road had been blacktopped.

But some things remain: the cattails and ripples still play along the shore. And at times, if you listen carefully, in between the calls of the crows and jays, and the warblers' songs, you may hear the laughter of the two oarsmen as they row into the lake and back to shore again and again, calling "Might as well get in" and "Might as well get out."

There was another ritual at the lake the summer Todd was three and four.

After the workout rowing the boat, they would walk up a gentle slope to a partly shaded place under a great oak tree and between white birch and green spruce.

They made a rough table by placing two weathered boards on top of an old stump, and moved an old log in place for a bench. And then, with good appetites from all the rowing, they picked huckleberries. The father sat on the log, holding some of the berries outstretched in his hand under the table. Todd, now a chipmunk, would scamper under the table and eat the berries.

"Oh, something's tickling my hand," the father would whisper, and pull it up to see that some of the berries were missing. "I wonder where those berries went?" Todd would peek out from under the table and squeak, "*I* don't know." He was able to keep a straight face for about three seconds. Then he would hold out a berry or two left in his hand. They did it again and again, each time laughing at the father's surprise that the berries were gone and wondering how it happened.

Sometimes, when the father "discovered" it was Todd, the chipmunk, who had eaten the berries, he would chase him and pick him up for a big hug and then they would roll in a grassy hollow. It was soft there and the dry grass was warm and fragrant from the summer sun.

Then they slid down a leaf-covered path to the beach and he lifted up Todd, now a bluebird, and held him as high as he could and Todd flew away up in the red pine branches. The bluebird was trying to whistle those long, happy summer days.

Back down to earth again, they walked a trampled path through tall green reeds to the water's edge. Todd would find a twig and throw it into the lake.

They would stand there quietly a long time watching the twig bob in the water and the ripples widen far out into the lake and others circle back to shore. They wondered what fish saw them and how long it took the ripples to touch the far shore.

Now, these years later, the father is the ripple, the fish, and the far shore.

There were other games and other days: horsey back rides like the ones the father's own father gave him on his way to bed. Todd found the ride to bed could be prolonged by directing his horse to visit various places in the house, and they would name these places mountains rather than steps, and ponds instead of sinks or bath tubs, and grass rather than rugs.

And when they were outside and Todd wanted to go faster, his horse would bend down and Todd would pick up a twig or flower stem, but instead of whipping his horse to speed up, Todd would tickle his horse behind the ear or along the neck. Then the horse would twist his head and make a horse-like sound and run on to escape any further tickles.

The father was sometimes the horse inside a small corral fenced in with sticks and branches. Often the horse would try to escape from the corral and the boy would go after him with a stick and herd him back into the corral. The horse would lie down and pretend to sleep, and the boy would touch him with another stick until the father, startled, jumped. The boy laughed and then of course they had to do it all over again.

They spent long hours running with kites, dangling sticks in water, with or without hooks or lines, and rolling inner tubes down a hillside. They worked together putting up a tire swing under an apple tree. The father pushed the boy away up into the sky where the green and yellow and brown leaf clouds sent shade to their playground.

Indoors, the boy often helped the father with the dusting and sweeping and washing up, and then they made things, like the time they made small boats with scraps of wood for the boy to sail in the bath tub called White Lake.

They made toy bulldozers with empty thread spools and rubber bands and a little wax and some used wooden match sticks. They played songs on instruments made from combs and toilet paper. Old and used things could always be salvaged: old roller skates could be nailed on a two-by-four with an old apple or pear box nailed upright to make a scooter.

Then there were the winter toys: one could step onto old tin cans, locking them onto the bottom of one's shoes and make a pair of ice skates. Half the fun of these toys was working together to make them and seeing old scraps of wood and boxes and cans turn into toys.

Often the boy was in the father's study while the father was writing at the desk he had fashioned from a large flush door placed on the top of four orange crates, two at each end. The boy liked to play under the desk when the father put a sheet or blanket around the sides of the desk, screening in a little hut.

Later they worked together, father and son, repairing a porch, painting the house, building a shop. The boy carried the tools and learned their names and how to use the hammer and saw and square and file and paint brush.

They were good buddies, this father and son, and one did not move far before the other knew it and came along.

Sometimes they had serious talks together, such as how to take care of oneself and be careful crossing streets. They always said their prayers together before the bedtime story and sleep. The boy asked many other questions: where people and animals came from and where they went after they died, and if stars were people.

Once Todd asked his father, "Why do people die?" Then he answered his own question. "Oh, I know. They get too big for their houses."

Where the Stream Bends

JUST THE TWO of us, watching the patient fishing of the stilt-legged great blue heron, the wing whip of the mallards raised from the marsh grass, and stirred by the wild call of the loons from the still face of the great lake.

Sometimes the trout break through the glassed calm and take flies that skim and light here, and it is a good place for a man and his son to walk and wait and flycast for the trout.

The stream is deepest here at the bend where the arc and swirl of the current scour the bottom in this last loop before falling down the shallow beach slope into the great lake. The stream has come winding many miles through cedar swamp and, rising over silted banks and washing through mulched lowlands, has darkened to the colour of tea.

At the mouth of the stream, the last fall, it blends with the lake in mixtures of blue and green and brown and cool and cold and sand and silt. And the tea water pours into the colder clearer great lake when the rolls ebb, and then, diluted, is partly poured back again with the throw of the waves. A light southeast wind strokes the stream in ripples above deep water where I know hungry trout wait, here where the stream bends.

I am here with Todd. We have left our fly rods back at the cabin.

"Should I go back for the rods?" Todd asks.

I don't answer right away. I'm not thinking of fly rods. "We could, but somehow ..." and I turn away and tilt the side of my sandal soles into the sand, making an x beside a piece of driftwood. "Somehow it seems all right just to be here, not to fish." It is quiet except for the low splash of waves at the shoreline. In a minute I add, "We could cast for bigger fish." I miss him already. He'll soon be going for his army physical exam and then military service.

"Hmm?" Todd asks, bending his head for a closer look at my face.

I turn toward the west, looking beyond a far point jutting into the lake, a point where layered shale holds heavy to the lake thrust. "The sunset, for instance. The big Rorschach in the sky, shapes of all kinds of things."

He turns. "I *do* see a fish there. Look, the dark clouds, over there." He is pointing. "The fins, and there's the head, and an eye too."

"Good catch," I say, and then I look down where tufts of dune grass have blown and twisted low to scribe the sand in slices and circles, resembling something like a beginning calligraphy lesson; but because the grass and wind alone have done it, there seems design and even miracle in it.

"What're you thinking about, Dad?"

"Oh, I don't know," I stall, "too much to single out right now, I guess," and I try to pull some courage in on a deep breath, and exhale sad thoughts of how it will be when he leaves and I am here alone.

I know when the time comes I will let go, I will screen my sadness when he goes away to the military service. And later let him go to a wife and have his own family and house, and a tent to follow a vacation we often took together. I know I can do what is hard to do, if I know it will be good for him. I have done it these many years and I will not change now.

I want to continue as a good father, and there are times now when I would like to relent and relax a little and be as needful and vulnerable as I feel; and to let Naomi into our lives to care for us as Todd and I care for each other, and for her to experience our caring for her as well.

Naomi transforms every place and experience she touches. I long for that and know the transformation extends to Todd as well. It is not just for me. I think of the carefully selected items of food or clothing she has sent or brought to us here at the lake while she has continued to live in the city. Her place is here, for all of us. She has even offered to continue working so Todd can go to the university.

But I am afraid to talk with Todd about my plans for marriage to Naomi, for fear he will feel I am abandoning him for her.

"Well, the sun's going down on the beach, and I want to see it. I'm going up the big dunes," and he reaches over and touches my arm. He starts his run and turns after twenty feet or so, calling back, "Remember, you used to time me?"

My "yes" is more to the boy I used to time than to Todd now. I sit on a fallen stump and watch him climb the dunes, slowing as it steeps near the top. Two crows caw out of the paperwhite birch.

"The sun sets later up there," I say quietly. "And later in his life," I add in a minute when the gathering coolness of the shading beach gives me a momentary shiver.

I walk over to the stream and see the ripple from a big one moving away into deeper water.

"He gave me an opening, Mr. Trout, 'What're you thinking about?' he said. I lied, 'I don't know.' I know all right and I can tell it all if I had the guts. Do you hear me, Mr. Trout? Do other fathers and mothers feel this way? I don't think they do, but I must be wrong. I couldn't be the only one. But he's going away, a new experience, the first step for going into the army. I don't want him sad, thinking of my being sad here when he leaves."

I rephrase it over and over as I might tell it to him later but fear I won't.

"There were many opportunities I missed in the past, not telling you how I felt, afraid of hurting you. Those were mistakes, however well-intentioned.

"Now I have a new time, a now time, to tell you how much I love you and Naomi also. I think she has proven her love to us in so many ways: all the mitts and wool sweaters and socks, the baking and preserves, the surfboard for you, on and on, and how she cooks and bakes for us up here. But when I sing her praises I am afraid you might think I am abandoning you for her. It is the love that she brings to us that I want for both of us. I am sorry for the hurt and the wrongs of my first marriage. I know that Naomi can show us what a loving wife and mother can really be for both of us."

Can I share these words and feelings with him?

What is there in our close relationship that avoids the sharing of sadness — father and son who have lived alone together for all but the first three of his eighteen years? Now as our first long separation approaches, we find ourselves mumbling and silenced and can fashion no language to deal with it, no words to plumb its depth and darkness.

I know he needs strength eventually to break free of me and have his own life, but I shudder and tighten, out of breath, at the prospect of hurting him in the process.

It is a sadness, it seems, I will never give full vent and voice to, for it would overwhelm me to know that it is sadness. Now it comes, as always, as a sweetness, bittersweet perhaps, but surely not all bitter. It is rather that I do not want to take the sweet too steadily, too deeply, lest I drain it, empty it, and we are left with only the bitter. I must husband them both, for they are both true and together they are most true.

There were times when I had rehearsed it so much it almost broke out of its own script. But I kept it well covered, that sadness, the fears. Or so I thought.

The words were starting out and I was holding

the force of them back deep in my throat. The control I had was faltering and the words were too even to be natural. The breathing was rising and falling and the words held taut in a line.

One time, just once, I did start to say it. We were coming back from a camping vacation, going up the incline of the overpass above the road to the house where he was born. The road was taking my thoughts out from under me, taking them along that road to the house I remembered. I started to say some things about life in that house. I wanted to say more than the few words I got out.

I pulled the car to the right and stopped, looking over the guard rail into the distance. "We lived down that road five miles. It was a little house. We had some good times there, but ..."

He looked in that direction, to the north, the right, looking and not yet knowing what I was saying. "But we had fun together, you and me. I'll have to get out that picture of you in the snow, your snowsuit, the snowman we made together."

He was restless. He might have picked up some anger in me that I had never sorted out from all I had suffered those years, in that place. Or sadness. I thought he didn't know how I had suffered and I suppose I made the decision then for him that he did not want to know, ever, and that he would hold it against me, anything I said about her.

"It was hard, Todd, but we made it, we loved

each other, the two of us." He turned in the car, frowning and restless, when I dared to look. I knew he did not want to hear it, anything about that time or about his mother.

And then I put a cap on saying any more, a firm lid on it. I knew my emotions would run away with it, and he must have heard all I did not say. He might have suspected there was some private pain there that I wanted to keep and yet somehow also wanted discovered, laid bare. When I looked over to him I saw him turn and wince and stiffen and I stopped. I tried to change the subject, to cheer him. He was frowning, more than frowning, and pulling away from me and he had not moved.

I stopped saying it then and there was so much more to tell. We were moving again then and going downhill. The car was driving itself and I was back there, back in the little house.

And so I took it all back within me to keep deep there. He wouldn't have known what to do with it, I thought later. I've lived alone with it. Only my pillow at night siphons off some of the locked melancholy of it.

From the dune top Todd's blue sweat shirt brightens from the sun. He stands tall, his fingers cupped and circling at each eye, as if looking through binoculars. "I see the island," he shouts down the long sand dune.

"How about the sunset?" I have to shout it twice.

"Great, but the fish is gone."

"And the sun is gone from here," I whisper, "and the warmth is going."

Todd stands a few more minutes and then leaps off into the loose sand, sliding, sinking in, then pulling his feet out to slide again. I think he might even roll down in the sand as he has many times as a youngster, on other hills and years ago, but he keeps upright.

My watching becomes staring and I go back to last winter and see snow and he is on his toboggan, standing, steadied by the rope he holds to the front. It is a cold and still night and the moon is bright and we puff breath out like steam locomotives as we laugh.

I walk toward Todd nearing the bottom of the dune. We meet at the path that threads back to the cabin, through trees partly covered at their bases with sand blown from the dunes and caught here. Some cedar and jack pines have browned at the tops and others are dead. Some are still green, with the same weight of sand at their crown.

From some storehouse where courage and hesitation mingle as they rise and fall, I open my mouth on the courage rise. "I've been thinking again about Naomi, about being engaged, getting married someday ... I guess I hesitate because you ... and I ... have been ... alone ... together ... so long. That's been great, but you might even like your own family and house some day. I wonder if I take the step first if it will be easier for you, in time. If that's what you would want to do."

He has been looking at me sideways and now when I face him he looks down. "No one has to decide anything today," I say, thinking I am taking both of us off the hook for now.

"And meanwhile, if we all live here together, Naomi has said she would work so there would be money for your university education if you want to go." He looks away, bends over to pick up a piece of driftwood, turns it over and tosses it down, then takes another piece and studies it.

We stop to pick the few blackberries left where our path opens out to the dirt road. "Mmm, still sweet," I say.

"I'm glad we've had the whole year up here, even though it's ending," and his voice drops off as he reaches over and gives me a few berries, deep, ripe, bursting to be eaten.

To reach the few berries left, we move beyond the grass trampled earlier in a path around the bushes. In the distance a car horn sounds, remote now, fading, as if driving off the edge of a dream sequence I'm waking from.

I've always had to work at not protecting Todd too much, letting him fall and get up again, holding myself back. Driving to his grade school years ago during many lunch hours at work, standing in the shade of the big maple tree by the school fence, under and between low-hanging branches, watching after he told me of fights at noon hour, stones thrown, tripping. Just watching, and then going back to my work after the lunch hour, to the lunch I hadn't eaten.

Someone finally reported me to the police for loitering around the playground, "watching the children in a suspicious way."

I was startled the day an officer came up behind me by the schoolyard fence. "You've been reported hanging around the playground watching the children. Looking for someone?"

"The boy in the red sweater? That's my son." It seems enough to say and not soil it, what I'm thinking. "He has nightmares about playground fights. Thought I could help him if I just saw what's going on over here."

"We have to be careful," and the officer turned to see where all the squealing was coming from. "That's for your kid's sake as well as all the other kids."

"I know. I appreciate that."

"You might want to talk to the principal or the boy's teachers. If they knew maybe they could help."

I did go in and talk with the principal, and checked to make sure they still had my phone number in case of emergency. I felt better.

Then listening to Todd at night when he told me as much as he wanted to say, knowing how much he kept back and that he needed time to tell all of it.

And the difficulty I had the day his school called when Todd broke his arm on the playground. The trouble I had getting out of the parking lot with all the cars coming in, and finally going over the curb and bending the muffler and tail pipe to get out and to the hospital.

Then holding back, holding in, swallowing dry and hard. Rushing, running, and then just before his room in the hospital, stopping, composing, breathing deeply, smiling. But not clever enough that a seven year old didn't see through it. Going in to his hospital room to give him courage and confidence, and the love in his eyes giving them all back to me. And then, together planning for all the names he could get on the cast on his arm.

Then later trying to recall if I'd combed his hair that morning of the day he broke his arm; and wondering if I'd waved to him as I always did just as he turned the corner on his way to school. Was I too busy that morning to do these things or am I now just tormenting myself with blame for what happened to him on the playground?

But time and control are slipping from my hands. Todd will be going away in a week for his army physical examination. Naomi has sent for more information for an overseas teaching post, wanting to be ready if we don't get married.

Now in Naomi's last visit before Todd leaves for the physical, I sense time running past me. We walk the beach and through a cut in the dunes to the calm of a sandhollow sloped to the sun. Naomi finds a dragonfly struggling for its life. Gently she picks it up, breathes softly on it cupped in her hands. Revived, it flies away.

"I feel revived like that when I'm with you. We could be so happy together." I take her hands in mine. "Parts of my life have been dormant, almost dead, but I stall and hesitate to do anything about it." And then in a moment, add, "Even talk about it."

"You don't have to talk about it."

"I want to, now. It's time. I feel so pulled, torn. I know it's my own doing." I hear a train whistle in the distance, three of the four blasts, and I wait for the fourth. I guess the wind has carried it in another direction or it blended in with the third.

"When you're here I want to spend time with you, but then I think Todd feels neglected, maybe jealous because we're always together when you're not here. So I try to shuttle back and forth sometimes. I know it's foolish." The train is closer and I pick up all of the whistle.

"You're too hard on yourself. You can be proud of what you've done for Todd."

"I want to do more for you now, for all of us. And yet as soon as I've said it, even now, I pull back from it, as if I'm abandoning Todd, undoing all I've done for eighteen years."

"Some things can't be rushed," she says, "and this is one of them. I know if you don't do it right, our relationship will suffer."

"When I went out to the highway with you last May when you left for home, after one more good-bye, I hurried back to the lake, to be with Todd to make up in a way I guess for all the time you and I had been together. For a while I couldn't find him. Finally I saw him sitting on the dunes looking out to the lake. He seemed so alone. I walked away quietly, circling around the stream bend where I saw his footprints and then back to the cabin. He had a right to be alone for a while with his thoughts and feelings."

The next afternoon we have a swim in the lake, and afterwards I'm drowsy and move higher on the beach to lie down. Naomi takes a long walk past a second stream emptying into the lake, far along to the west. I see her go away and I see her come back.

But that night I dream of it and fear I'll be gone before she's back, gone somewhere into the dark of the clouded noon light, reflected off so many prisms of sand and water, stream and lake, that I'm lost, and when she comes I cry out of the silence but it's only a more profound and frightening silence I appeal to.

It's like trying to waken from a dream, a bad dream, straining to call or shout and knowing that no sound carries, that no one will ever hear me. I see Naomi turn and call and I call too but my voice is stuck in my throat and cannot be heard. Then I hear thunder and it begins to rain. When I waken I am soaking with perspiration.

The next evening Todd climbs the dunes and Naomi walks alone into a setting sun. I stand on the beach waving first to one and then the other and wonder if it matters to either that they see what I am doing.

It has always been hard to think of living here in the cabin without Todd or living anywhere without him after all our years alone together. Now it is equally hard to think of living anywhere or at all without Naomi as my wife. But if I marry how will it be with the three of us living together? I suspect I have worked myself into a box. I see it is triangular shaped.

"Well, let's get out of the cabin," I say. "How about a walk through the woods and along the beach to the point? It's a great afternoon." And then looking at Todd, I add, "for all of us." Todd probably sees I still have not given up the idea of his coming back to live here after military service.

It's June and the black flies and mosquitoes drive us from the woods onto the beach. We walk to the place where the stream bends and it's like the other time when the trout broke the smooth surface to take flies. We stop and look into the stream depths at the bend where it is deepest.

"It's so peaceful here," Todd says.

Still its deep tea colour, a lot of water has flowed down the stream since that afternoon when we walked here together. For a while it colours and warms a small part of the great lake. And then, slowly but surely, it mixes and flows on, changed but not lost.

Naomi and I walk to the second stream one afternoon. "It is said," I begin, "that 'faint heart never won fair lady,' and I want to thank you for your patience. I propose but then I also oppose, that is, itemize the laundry list of objections to our getting married in the near future." I turn around and see Todd sitting on a log near the water's edge, sitting there alone where he and I have often sat together, for the log holds two or three. "There is the big problem now, Todd is sitting back there so alone."

"I see him so clearly in my inner eye, I don't actually have to look back," Naomi says. "But come on," and she takes my arm and swings me around with her to face back to Todd, "let's go back and have him walk with us. Or go in swimming together, or play ball on the beach, anything together."

"Won't it be so obvious what we're doing?" I ask.

"Maybe, but what's wrong with that? I think it's time we speak up and speak out. And that means me too." As we near Todd, Naomi waves her arms for him to join us.

"Well, Todd, I hope you'll tell me if it's okay to come back for you, to want you on this walk with us, the three of us together."

"We don't always have to walk together, any of us." I add. "But we were along the beach there thinking of you and wanting to be with you, both of us, so we thought we'd come back and tell you … and ask you … How about it?"

"Sure," and his feet are moving and he is looking up, pointing. "Watch the loons now, coming in for a landing."

A few days later they are both gone. On her way home Naomi drives Todd to the city for his army physical. I stay alone at the cabin to sort out feelings of Todd going away. Walking the beach, walking the woods, walking, walking, until finally I prepare myself for a new life with Naomi.

When Todd comes home for three days after his physical, he's ready to be my best man. Naomi and I are married in an old stone church eight miles away, the pews wooden stalls with hinged doors. Naomi is beautiful in the long white gown that she made herself. I think Todd returns to his army training satisfied that I am not living alone.

When we talk about having a baby, Naomi almost convinces me that it's as much her own desire as concern for me that we not have a baby. Then I find a note she has written to herself. I'm looking for a recipe, intending to surprise her with a favorite goulash upon her return from town. The note is in her recipe file.

> *Channing has given so much of his*
> *life in raising Todd, and was so*
> *saddened when Todd left for the army*
> *exam. They have a rare relationship,*
> *beyond comparison. A baby would be*
> *another triangle. I love him too much*
> *to—*

And it ends. I do not say anything about the note when she comes back, but she might think my hug especially energetic.

The Slow Tide
of Nightfall

FROM THE DINING ROOM Channing hears the creak of the rocker as his son Todd rocks back and forth in the adjacent living room. Channing begins to pick up some vague danger that the rocking signals to him. For the past hour he has sensed something tracking him, moving around him and then away again.

It's a fall Saturday evening. Channing's wife Naomi has been gone since noon, visiting her sister across the city. She put some things for supper in the slow cooker, chicken and potatoes and carrots, so that supper would be easy for them to fix. She'll be gone until ten or eleven.

Channing looks out the window at the darkening, and across the driveway toward the neighbour's house. Their dog barks from the house in the direction of the back fence. Someone may be going down the alley to or from the stores on Whitlock street. Channing can see the neon sign of the Rialto Tavern there, blinking on and off. He waits for the neighbour's dog to bark again, and still the Rialto sign blinks its red beacon. He hears the rocking again, creaking the floor.

The creaking stops and Channing turns toward the door. Todd is standing in the doorway as if gripped by some dread, but he doesn't say anything. He stands there, looking at his father but not focusing on him.

It had started earlier, outside, this afternoon when father and son were raking leaves across the front lawn and pruning some ragged branches on the birch clump. Todd was quiet, his thoughts miles away. And now in the kitchen, at supper, the strained silence continues. Todd usually wolfs down his potatoes, but tonight he mashes them with his fork again and again on his plate.

"Lumps?" Channing finally asks, mostly to interrupt Todd's hypnotic staring at his plate. They had taken great care to mash out all the lumps earlier, added warm milk and whipped them smooth.

"Huh? Oh, no." Todd takes a forkful and chews and chews, then picks at the chicken.

"You don't have to finish it."

In waiting for Todd's words Channing hears other sounds then, of knives and forks on plates and the loud tick of the old clock on the wall. Then more distant sounds, a car horn blowing down the street and a young child's voice calling along the sidewalk.

Channing sees Todd looking at him, a side glance that quickly veers away. Todd looks at the only blank wall in the room, unwilling to be distracted, or perhaps writing large there the words he cannot give voice to.

The sounds are forming in the restlessness of feelings stirring to be expressed and words shaping to be heard, but they are not audible yet.

Determined to break the awesome silence by simply opening his mouth and letting out whatever will come, Channing says abruptly, "Look at the purple grass." He has turned to look out the window at the front lawn. It seems a strange and inappropriate remark to break the silence.

"I mean, I've always wondered about paintings with purple grass and red and blue. But look," he points to the grass near the birch clump on the lawn. "It's not just the artist, but the sun and clouds and shadows from the trees and reflections from the windows. It's done with mirrors, magic."

Todd looks without seeing and they are silent again. The daylight retreats from the room, and a coolness and muted mauve touch the table and chairs. The slow tide of nightfall is flowing in.

Channing has been remarried for two years, ending a fifteen year stretch of batching it for the two of them. Todd has returned from military service and is living at home again. Yet their relationship "beyond compare," as a neighbour put it, has a flaw, a strange reluctance of either of them to share their concerns or worries with the other. Their very closeness exposes their sensitivities and seems a barrier to sharing pain. They share laughter and hopes, this father and son, but are painfully reticent about fears and sadness, screening and shaping them to protect each other.

Now at the supper table, Todd opens his mouth,

gasps in air and starts to form a word, and then falls away from it again into silence. And Channing doggedly pursues an alternating silence and then small talk, as if his minor maneuvers can somehow save them both from navigating a major one.

Todd usually goes upstairs to his room right after supper, and then within half an hour he comes down again, dressed to go out for the evening. Lately he has been going out almost every night, coming in about midnight. He is seeing Sheila, a girl he met a year ago at an A & W drive-in where she works. Whenever relatives or friends kid him, "When are you getting married?" he reacts with a "Never!" or "Who, me?"

Naomi and Channing have never met Sheila, but Todd has changed so much since meeting her that they are concerned. He has given up any idea of going on to college, keeps late hours, and spends all of his money as soon as he earns it. Later they concede they would probably have been critical of anyone as a potential wife for Todd.

As late as he stays out, Todd is usually up on time in the morning and off to his job on the line at General Motors. Both Todd and his father work there and ride together.

Tonight Todd does not go upstairs after supper. He sits at the table and Channing moves his dishes to the sink, relieved to be up and moving rather than sitting through more uneasy silence.

Todd carries his dishes to the sink, not putting them down for a long half minute, as he stares down into the sink. He turns then and walks to the stove. Channing runs the water until it is hot, and when he looks, Todd is still at the stove staring at the pilot light. He turns a knob and the flame from the pilot flicks over to the burner, and then he turns it off. He turns another burner on and off, then straightens the magnets on the fridge door.

It has happened before, this strain of something waiting to be said, and the tension building. When Todd was younger his father helped him speak up by saying it for Todd or kidding him, sometimes diverting the boy from what he wanted to say, so that he had said something else. It appears that this time Todd will not say anything else. He will wait to say it himself, and right, or he will say nothing at all.

If I can keep talking, maybe Todd won't have to say it, Channing thinks. *There won't be room for anything except my words and my concern that he is all right and nothing will change.*

Todd circles the kitchen, shuffles and leans, opens his mouth and closes it without speaking, flips the first few pages of the newspaper. Finally he moves into the living room and sits in the rocker, pushing himself back and forth in an anxious rhythm.

A picture comes to Channing's mind of other mothers and fathers sitting on the edge of their sons' or daughters' beds and hearing about their dates, their questions, their problems. *What's wrong with me?* Channing wonders. *Todd and I are so close and yet we don't talk anymore about painful things, or perhaps we never did. There are such gaps and paradoxes in our closeness.*

The phone rings, a welcome respite, an end-of-the-round bell for a rest, a breather. "There's no Gerry here. You have the wrong number," Todd says, and he hangs up. Channing thinks Todd might begin talking now that the silence has been broken. But the silence only seems more oppressive.

Have Todd's unspoken words been rehearsed in another time? Will they be voiced in another tongue or will they find expression somewhere else? From some long ago sandbox these grains of childhood were thrown, and through all the years they have defied falling. They seem to float back and forth as if suspended.

I want so desperately for some things to be that I strive to create a whole new world to put them in, and us at the center.

In all of this Channing is waiting to hear Todd's concern so he can make it *his* problem, one he can solve, one he can get right to work on. *I've helped him through the measles and chicken-pox, earaches and sprained ankles, through European history and algebra at school and, more recently, flat tires and fouled spark plugs. Why am I so useless now?*

It comes to Channing then that perhaps this is a problem he can no longer do anything about. The decision has been made, the die cast. There's nothing left for him to do but hear – or overhear – the conclusion.

Well, he's picked it up honestly, this way of not sharing problems. What problems have I shared with Todd? We laugh together but endure pain alone.

It was years before Channing learned from Todd's grandmother that his son's yearly birthday wish was always that his father's polio-paralyzed leg would get better. He wished it because Channing never faced him and said, "Todd, this leg is never going to be much different. I'm sorry, but I'm very lucky I can use it at all, that I can walk." Why hadn't he said that, and given Todd back all the wishes for himself, for bicycles and trains, toboggans and skis?

I never told him how shattered I was at the divorce, when Todd was three. And angry with myself that I hadn't taken action years earlier. Why I'd put up with her drinking, sure I was doing the right thing for Todd, and then wondering if it was all so wrong to have waited that long. I didn't dare say anything against his mother to him, but it was so much to bear myself all these years. It must have been a shock to Todd when I was engaged and then married. He had reason to believe it would always be just the two of us.

Channing thinks of the day he bought Naomi's ring. He'd known her since Todd was four. When he decided to marry, he thought it would be good to involve Todd, that he would be best man, that they could even go together to buy her ring. Todd had agreed to go downtown to the jeweler with his father, but when they got there he preferred to sit in the car. Walking along the sidewalk to the store, Channing kept looking back at Todd sitting alone in the car, thinking maybe he would get out and catch up to him. Todd seemed so alone and abandoned, Channing almost put off the engagement.

That night, seeing how hang-dog Channing was, Naomi almost called it off herself. Todd seemed to come to terms with the marriage, but several months after the wedding Channing found their wedding picture under a tray in Todd's toolbox, crumpled and torn.

In a trunk near Todd's toolbox, Channing saw the

plastic curtains they used before Naomi moved in and made curtains for all the windows and replaced the worn and colourless towels and sheets. Channing felt a strange melancholy in looking at these things and remembering the years he and Todd had lived alone.

Channing had never really allowed himself to admit how pained Todd must have felt about the wedding. Believing that Naomi would be a wonderful mother for Todd, Channing hadn't remained open for any objections from him. *I denied so much, feared so much, avoided so much.* Channing remembered saying some things about how their love would be multiplied rather than divided when Naomi moved in. More than arithmetic was needed to straighten that one out.

Todd matched his father's generosity with his own generosity. He would never take a last slice of bread or piece of fruit when he was with Channing. Neither would Channing, of course, and so they had to halve it or it would remain uneaten.

The wind rattles the storm window they worked on together last week-end. Channing hears the rocker find a loose floor board, and then the groan and squeak as Todd rocks back and forth. He doesn't move the rocker. Perhaps the groan is speaking for him.

Channing stays in the kitchen, hoping Todd will come back to talk. Then Channing goes to the desk in the dining room, and it is there he looks out the window to the neighbour's light and dog and the blinking neon sign.

He's there for perhaps ten minutes and the duet of rocker and floorboard stops. When he turns, Todd is at the dining room door. He is staring at his father yet right past him. His eyes are glassy, the pupils consuming the blue. Then the words come out, as if rehearsed for hours, forgotten and then retrieved and needing unscrambling. His right hand is clenched in a fist, his left fingers pick at hang nails, and his shoulders are hunched up in tension to crowd his neck. Channing remains quiet and finally Todd comes to the courage or desperation or simple recklessness he needs to say it.

"I want to get married," finally tumbles out, and for Channing it is like hearing the whistle of an artillery shell and waiting for it to hit. The threat has sounded but the damage is yet to be done. Todd has been unable to erase the hint of a question mark, so that later Channing will wonder whether he heard, "Can I get married?" or "I want to get married." The words are lost somewhere between them and neither of them will claim them. Channing feels the blood drain from his face, that it has turned to the white-gray shade of wood ashes.

Twenty-one years and we have come to this? Todd doesn't want to hurt me. That's why he circles and waits and rocks and chokes it in so long. But he has been hurting himself and he's hurting now. It's something he has to say because it's something he has to do. He wants me to know and to say it's all right.

This is the problem I've been waiting to hear, so I can get to work on it. But there's nothing for me to do now, only accept it, what he wants. It's all settled. Only my approval is wanted.

Channing doesn't say "congratulations!" nor that it's all right. He fears that Todd is going to do something too risky to survive, as if he's determined to swim the English Channel and all that's required of Channing is to pick out the time when he'll jump in.

There is no language between them to say such things, no words to plumb such depth or carry such weight. *That he has spoken at all is proof enough of his great need and desire, his desperation even, to marry. He won't be permanently side-tracked by my unspoken reservations. And I won't voice them now.*

The present and future are too painful for Channing to think of, so he reaches into the past for some comfort. He thinks of the first time Todd stood to walk.

He teeters, about to fall, but I don't go to him immediately.

"Come on, Toddy, that's a boy, come on." I prize this time with Toddy, standing, his first steps. "Oops, fall down, go boom, up again, atta boy." The next time he falls I cannot hold back. I crawl over to him, nudge my head into his tummy, hug him as I roll over on my back, suspend him over my chest, and then put him down again on his feet by the table.

It's four o'clock. Shadows fall across the floor, highlighting the worn spots, and start up the wall. I'll always remember this day. Someday he'll be gone, into the army, or to marry, but for today, "Here, Toddy, take my hand."

The phone rings. "Wrong number again, probably. Let it ring," but Todd has already turned to answer it.

Channing gets up and lowers the blind on the side window. Todd is planning to leave and all the little things of life still go on as if nothing has happened: a phone rings, a blind is lowered, a tree branch taps against the window.

"Yes, yes … I did … okay … half an hour … bye," Todd says and then hangs up.

So that's it, Sheila encouraged him to do this, to tell me about the marriage, and now the call is to make sure he's done it. He's said it, I know about it, there'll be no more delay. Todd has done what she asked and now he'll go to her and the break will be complete, all but the ceremony and moving out.

Todd goes upstairs from the phone. Channing hears him open and close his bedroom door, move the chair in his room, open his chest of drawers. They are sounds that will be silent in a while, when he moves. Channing knows he'll remember Todd standing in the doorway, their eating supper together, him flicking the pilot light over to the burner, and the creaking back and forth in the rocking chair, in the dark. These things will not be for long now. And yet they will always be, hauntingly. Todd will clear out his closet, drawers, things under his bed. But … *maybe he'll leave some things, and we'll keep the room as his room. It may take him forever to move out.* There are little hopes to build on.

Todd comes downstairs and to the dining room door again. Channing gropes for words and loses them as his thinking veers from them, rushing on ahead. He gets up from his chair and puts his arms out and they hug and pat each other on the back.

In hugging him, at first Channing still feels his

young boy. Then he realizes Todd is a man, the broad shoulders, the deep chest. If it seems a sudden change, it is perhaps that Todd's words have pulled the boy out of the man's body. "... want to marry ... marry ..."

However, it has been happening for years, of course, at first below the level of awareness, happening to this manchild in every cell and only later showing at the surface level. *When did he get older and where was I? When was he no longer a child, and what was I doing while it happened?*

Channing tries, but only feebly, to hide his sadness. He thinks Todd will see it. And then Todd turns, as if in response to another call than his father's, perhaps to a mating call, distantly heard but by then the stronger call. The juices flow in him that swamp everything else. He belongs not even to Sheila now but to the species.

It is a different world, a world where Naomi, and now Sheila, are necessary and important characters. It is by turns a frightening and an alluring world, this world of triangles, of sexuality. But it is a real world and its pull is strong and irresistible.

Channing hears Todd turn the key to lock the side door, slam his car door and start down the driveway. "There will be times," Channing whispers, "when he will visit and be leaving like this, with Sheila and ... a little Todd probably."

Channing walks to the front window and watches him drive down the street. Only when he gets to the corner and turns onto Whitlock does he hit the accelerator, and the mufflers roar.

Channing waits a long time by the window, looking

out to the lawn they raked and the tree they pruned. He tries to put Todd back on the lawn again, both of them there, Todd handing him a pruning saw and Channing holding the ladder steady as Todd climbs to a higher branch. Then an emptiness tells him he never wants to rake leaves again or care for the birch. His eyes scan blindly back and forth across the lawn, now emptied of Todd and himself.

Then something seems to move in him and he knows he will go on, that this will pass. He doesn't want it to pass but suspects that it will.

Channing turns to look at the rocker, quiet now and still, and thinks he hears the distant thunder of the mufflers.

Waiting

IT WAS the hour past the hour his dream had placed him there and he waited. She would come, and come beyond the hedge laced and winterset and through trees and around bushes outlined to the beige-bricked building where warm and lovely he knew she sat waiting this hour, waiting for him to come and then she would walk.

He forgot for a moment how she looked, and struggled to visualize how he expected her, to stem the rising panic of losing her if he lost the clear picture of her hair and eyes and lips. Then he released how he had expected her and saw her now as she came.

"I'll wear them some day when the weather warms."

"I don't want you to wear them for everyone to see, just me. Bring them in your bag."

It didn't matter. The words were remote now in a faraway time and a distant place. Swinging her bag, she came striding from her hips, throwing long legs to the gray tufted and brown winter grass. He looked and did not take his eyes from her. She was coming to him and that was all that mattered now.

She looked up and pointed her walk to him. Their eyes met a distance still long enough to let the focus drift, to look aside or beyond each other, he to those walking near her or the backdrop of trees and buildings, and she to cars passing or the drab gray mural of semi-detached residences across the street.

She pointed her stride to him around the hedge end and across the walk and the remaining grass now and he reached for the door. Getting in the car, she put one nyloned knee on the seat and leaned over to kiss him. The winter cold of her forehead and cheeks warmed; her lips full and red; he held her a moment and then they drove away and she moved closer beside him.

He turned and she was watching him as she always did to catch his mood. He was glad his dream had wakened him for this.

He knew not to ask where she wanted to go but drove. He took her hand and looked at her and back at the road. When there were no cars coming, he leaned over and she turned her face and their lips met.

"I missed you, Carol."

"It was only a day. I missed you too, Dan," and her shoulder and thigh tightened against his.

She moved her bag over to the passenger's door and turned her face back. Her lips parted and she did not smile. She continued looking at him and knew he liked that look. She put her head against his shoulder. "Mother's going home Thursday." She was not looking at him but she felt him stir and could picture his eyes pulling narrow and his lips spreading lightly in a smile.

It had not started this way. It had started in a white house under rain skies. The alarm sounded. Lois reached over and turned it off. A light rain-loped breeze moved the curtain. She looked at Dan and he was staring at the ceiling. He wasn't stretching or yawning as he usually did when first waking. He was mumbling something about divorce and she did not ask him what he had said.

I waited until the children were grown. He wanted to be able to say it, to know he had waited and done it that way, waited and done it right. As right as something so wrong could be.

The children, Jim at twenty-three, and Sue at twenty-one, could outspend and outrun him and would surely outlive him.

It was musing on being outlived that disturbed him: not outlived by his children, nor Lois, but by desires and dreams and some designs he had on a different life, different in ways he would never realize if he did not follow the stirring inside him. He brooded and the darkness in him grew.

It is not enough to be a father, soon a grandfather, and have a grandmother-wife, to have son and daughter and job and car and home. It is all fine but it is no longer enough. What I want is life now, wrenched free of distractions and impediments and accoutrements, my life lean to living to being to me. I can feel the slender lure of it, the seductive call of it. To get off the detour finally and onto the main and true and straight and narrow path of it. To feel the purr and softness and the stirring rage of it too, and to answer while there is yet force and drive and piss and vinegar in it.

Now it is my turn. He started with that. He did not want to hurt Lois. He was willing for her to have a turn now too; for she too had sacrificed. She was only momentarily set back when Jim and then Sue had moved out and married.

"It doesn't seem to bother you, the kids gone."

"Oh, I look forward to grandchildren."

"Baby sitting them? I'm not ready for that," he moaned.

His own adolescence passed in review, caring for ill parents and a younger brother, denying himself, putting off until later.

Bewildered by cross-currents of desire and denial, in line for his turn now without knowing which way to turn, Dan grew more irritated than independent. He picked quarrels with Lois to justify reactions he was building to. But with each argument against Lois, he silently offered one in her favour when she made no rebuttal. He did not want to leave Lois, but he did not want to give up Carol either.

Lois wanted to hold on to what had always been, had been for twenty-five years. Now, just the two of them, they had a chance to do some things together they had put off while the children were home. She still had a good figure, but Dan didn't seem to look at her much anymore. She got a new bathing suit and modeled it for him. "Do you like it?" He mumbled something about it being too late and walked out of the room. He denied himself any pleasure in looking at Lois, as if somehow disloyal to Carol.

"Dan Wilkins! You come back here!" And he did, a bit sheepishly. "If you think I'm going to freeze in this bathing suit, what there is of it," and she looked down and ran her finger under a flimsy part of it, "without one of your warming hugs, you've got another thought or two coming."

Dan came back on the edge of his regrets that he had pouted and walked out, and was grateful to Lois for preventing the guilt that would have followed such petulance.

Lois knew that she could be wrong, that he might already have made up his mind to leave her, and he just needed some provocation to do it with a measure of guilt he could live with. She was determined not to give him that measure.

Whatever he has to do, he will have to do alone. If there was both love and fear in her reaction, she expressed the love and let the fear seep down inside her, giving her a weakness she had not known before. She sensed she was making it easier for him to do it, by her passivity, by what he might take as her permission, by the assurance that he still had her love.

Lois knew that Dan would not go with her for marriage counselling, so she went alone. "Get out more. Have a life of your own. Get him to sit up and take notice," the counsellor said. She began to consider that, but when he suggested she have an affair of her own, and they have their interviews at his apartment, Lois walked out in disgust. She was in tears by the time she got to her car.

Son Jim called Lois one afternoon and then went over to see her. "I hate to carry tales, Mother, but I've seen this going on too long to ignore it any more."

"I've known about it too, Jim. I don't believe your father thinks he's fooling me, nor do I feel like a fool. I haven't said anything because often when something is said it marks it indelibly in someone's mind and makes it harder to work out."

"I could give you details."

"Details are for proof, for building a case. Proof sets things in concrete. I'm not after that. I look for things to change, a phase he's going through perhaps."

"Some phase!"

"You and Sue went through many trying stages when you were growing up. By not making a big issue out of them, I was happy to see you both go *through* them rather than get stuck in them. I want your father to have the same passage if possible."

"You seem so cool about it. Father's running around and you're so, so philosophical about it."

"I'm not a woman of steel. I'm as upset and concerned as you are, more I'll bet, but I want to control my reactions and keep my eye on the goal. I'm not really as cool as that sounds, but it's the reaction I'm striving for right now."

"You're something else, Mother," and he hugged her.

"Thanks, Jim, for coming to me. It took a lot of courage and love to do it."

"More courage than I had for months."

For Dan there was duty and responsibility in his

marriage, musts and shoulds and oughts. There was sameness and boredom and irritation too. But when he was with Carol, it was exciting. He did not have to work at it. He admitted that Carol was not as attractive as Lois. What was it? What was this intensity he had for Carol? It called beyond reason and good judgment and time and control, and it controlled him. He knew he would not give Carol up. Yet he also feared that later he would regret such stubborn foolhardiness. The aching yearning for her continued.

"Coming back from Toronto I saw a log house, lots of trees around it and a big mill wheel beside a stream that ran across the back of the acreage. I thought of our living there and how peaceful it would be." She was showing him her dreams.

There were days when pain was the only constant. Despite gentle and persistent pleas from Carol, Dan would take no steps to leave Lois. They knew, Carol and Dan, they would go through other seasons and it would be as unending and cyclic as it had been. They would rise and fall with the winds and ebb and flow with the tides and warm and cool with the days and the nights and the seasons. There would be nothing even and the same about it, nothing tranquil.

It would change with them and they with it, this relationship of intense possessiveness one moment and flight and denial the next. Dan fled from Lois to Carol and from Carol to Lois, from dissatisfaction to satiety and back, questing, finding, losing. They knew they owed their love to the winds of many moods, Carol and

Dan. If they were becalmed, they feared it would be fatal. It seemed that only in threat and risk and danger, even deceit, could they survive together.

With Carol now he drove until vacant lots outnumbered houses, smaller shacky houses in clusters, then fewer houses and small farms whose owners commuted to the city factories and farmed part-time. Then larger farms with red and yellow-bricked farmhouses and outbuildings jutting, angled, attached like dominoes abandoned by children off to play another game. The fence rows were bushed and treed without fences, reining in winter wheat or fields plowed for spring planting.

Three crows lifted from a harvested cornfield, black kites borne to the sky, and then, after a half dozen flaps of their large wings, settled back down when the car passed.

He drove on, and nearing the lake the farms were split again into smaller acreages, and then cottages, many boarded up for the winter. He slowed and turned into a sandy lane, entrance to a small park. An old blue and white bus sagged off the lane, its sides pocked with peeling red-lettered signs for another season: "Pop Corn" and "Pop" and "Candy".

They parked and got out and walked toward the lake frozen and silent.

"Not like last July," he said. "Remember?"

"Or next July." She ignored the past and would answer only to the future.

They walked along the beach and he held her and they warmed each other in the cold and the night unfolding. Dan felt a strangely comforting security in walking the stiff and barren beach and being adrift as the darkness seeped through the dampness.

"This afternoon at home I felt so alien to all my things, possessions, the house, furnishings. They crowded me. I felt they were trying to bind me, possess me." He pulled Carol to the side and they walked around a fallen log on the beach. "I feel freer, away from it all." Some willows low hanging and taller poplars, although bare of leaves, pulled a darkening curtain as they walked farther on the beach, lending in his thought an air of fantasy that this path led somewhere, somewhere new, somewhere promising. He tightened his arm around her waist. "We could just walk away."

She looked at him and then away. "Or drive, if you want to be more practical," he added, sensing something critical rising in her. "We could head south ... waarm," he dragged out the word. She stiffened. "I frighten you with that talk, don't I?"

"No. Not if it were possible, if you were serious." She spoke softly, confidently, but more to herself, and ended by whispering, "If it came true." She struggled in her mind to get a quotation right, something about castles in the air being all right, just be sure to put foundations under them. But some irritation intervened, as if a quotation would be setting her feelings aside for someone else's words. She looked up at Dan to see if there was any trace of hope for the dream coming true.

He sensed her expectation, stopped and kissed her. It was not enough. She had wanted some words from him to help her hope survive, and he had not found the words.

He knew his dream was feeble, even comic in comparison to hers. He wanted to dream it again and then will it to be so. To try and do that. To let the dream and love transform him even as they had transformed her.

Opening his coat he took a scarf from his inside pocket. He turned to her and put it over her head and tried to tie it under her chin. "There, what are they called, 'bushkas', something like that, Russian probably, how do you spell it?"

She laughed. "You got part of it. It's babushka. I think I'll just have the scarf," and she pulled it down around her neck. "You can spell that all right."

He missed her good-natured reaction, still trying to hold his fantasy. He feared it would fade if he were distracted for a moment. His attentiveness with the scarf was from a dream sequence. How strong was a dream so simply distracted, so easily derailed, he wondered.

Tammy's words came back to him. It was years ago, twenty-five, six? Half a lifetime. She was wise, Tammy. When he told her he loved her, she looked at him quizzically. It was not Carol's look. "You just think you're in love with me," Tammy had said. "You're really in love with love, and I just happened by."

She had put it gently and her beautiful eyes smiled on it and on Dan. She could have said it differently, more crudely, as he did to himself when he understood her finally, years and experiences later. She could have said it was a mating call, not a romantic lyric he was responding to.

He had denied it, vehemently, he recalled. The idea was preposterous. That his ardent profession of love could as readily have been directed to any number of other women at that moment. Could it be so now, with Carol, that he wanted to love someone, to be loved by her, and so he created her to love and she was transformed by that love?

And Lois, he thought, what about Lois? How does she fit into this neat theory? Lois, who loves me so well. Thinking of Lois stiffened him to going any farther.

"Far enough," he said, and tightening his arm around Carol, he swung a U-turn to head back.

"We could just walk away," she parodied. She looked about as if searching for something, in the trees, in the clouds, and then cupped her two hands by her eyes, resembling binoculars, "or did I miss it somehow, the dream castle we were walking to?"

"Ouch! Touché!"

Looking ahead against the lights of a boat livery bait house, they saw someone standing on the beach by the lane they had come down. Standing there and then seeming to dart back out of sight into the trees and bushes at the edge of the beach. They were bare and leafless, the trees and the bushes, but still thick enough to screen the person at that distance.

"Someone on the beach," he said, glad for the interruption.

"Gone now."

"Guess his ship wasn't coming in tonight after all."

"Or hers."

"Yes, or hers." He was cautious, listening, watching as they walked back. He did not want anyone to surprise them. He felt protective of her. He could fight or just give up his wallet, his watch. But he did not want her to be hurt, involved. Involved, that was it. If something happened and it was reported to the police, their names would be in the paper. They heard a car start up, saw headlights flood the beach and swing in an arc and then dim and disappear. And the car louder when it left the lane and sped off along the black top.

"Let's not go yet," she said when they got into the car and he pulled the keys from his pocket. She turned and leaned against the door on her side. "Can we talk?"

"Talk? Sure." He pushed the knobs down to lock both doors, then turned and leaned against the door, his left arm on the steering wheel.

"I guess I want to know."

"Know?"

"Know what we are going to do."

"Do?" He knew he was sounding dense, guarded.

"About us. And if you say 'us?' I'll ..."

"We can stay," and he put his right hand up as if to ward off a blow from her. He slipped the key in the ignition, "but I'll start it up and get the heater going."

"Maybe it's the impossibility of it that makes it so attractive," and she turned her head and blew on the window. "For you anyway." She ran her gloved hand through the light moisture gathered there. The window cleared. "Its appeal and excitement. And also the fear, knowing it may never go anywhere."

"We've made no promises, we're breaking no vows."

"Not before a priest, we haven't, but surely to ourselves. Our *seeing* each other at all is a vow, a promise, a hope … and more …" She felt stronger now and sensed his weakness. It was not a weakness in answering her, a weakness of words only, of argument. It went deeper than that and she pushed against it.

"What if," she started, turning to look full at him, "what if I told you I'd set up an appointment with a lawyer for tomorrow morning at 10, to get your divorce started? 10 A.M."

He had his window open an inch, a guard against fumes with the engine running, and he heard a cracking noise. "What's that? Sounds like someone in the bushes."

"Oh, it's probably Len. He's been tailing me lately."

"You never said anything before." He turned around to look out the window. "That was him, earlier, on the beach, wasn't it?"

"Yes, he loves playing detective."

"Why didn't you tell me?" Now Dan wasn't sure if it was Len or his own son Jim whom he'd also seen playing detective, on other occasions.

"He's harmless. You worry so." She opened the door and got out.

"Carol, don't get out there. Get in the car!" Dan got out his side. A car started up and pulled away.

"He's gone now. I told you he's harmless."

"I still think you should have told me."

"Why? Would it make any difference … between us?"

"No. No! But we should be careful." They got back in the car. Dan turned the heater up to high.

"What about the lawyer at 10 tomorrow?"

"You didn't." He pulled his left arm off the steering wheel and reached toward Carol.

"Of course I didn't. But what if I had?" Dan's arm went back on the steering wheel. "See, already it takes the force out of it, your knowing it isn't so. You don't have the same pressure to speak your real feelings. I don't mean you lie. It's just that ..." and she wanted to get it right, "... that you can give a make-believe feeling or answer to a make-believe situation. But if it were a real situation then the real ..." and she trailed off, feeling foolish for having to finish it, spell it all out. Anyone could see it.

He felt she had devalued him in not finishing her point. He knew what she was going to say. He could finish it himself. The slight was in her not saying it. He was pushed to take his strength back, to answer himself as well as Carol.

"We make impossible demands on love." His voice was lower. "It makes impossible demands on us, and we *deliver* those impossibilities. We become, for a day or month or year, what we have not been before. What we have not done before, what was untouched, undreamed maybe, impossible ..." and he paused, "we do, because of love."

"Yes, yes," and she was caught up in it, but only momentarily, for she went on with it, on beyond the dream and impossible possibility of it, and back to what she had first asked, wanting to know what they were going to do. "And is the lawyer at ten an impossibility? Maybe it is," and she answered her own question because she didn't want to hear his answer, his evasion. She wondered if she had pushed too far but could not bring herself to retreat. Not now. Not yet.

"I'm sorry, it's disappointing. You've waited, very patiently ..."

She expected him to add "... until now," but he was quiet and took her hand. "But sometimes I wonder what we're waiting for," she said.

"If we're just waiting for Montreal or Paris or whatever, and don't have anything along the way going there, it might not be so much when, if, we finally get there."

"Motherhood and apple pie!" and she did not try to mask the sneer.

"What?"

"What you said. Who can dispute it? And what does it have to do with what we're talking about, except in such a general way as to be useless?"

"Okay."

"Don't sound so crushed. I mean, we always veer off into general statements. The lawyer at ten is not at all general."

He had looked at his watch several times and was tapping his feet.

"Nor is going home now, you to yours, me to mine," she said, turning now from leaning on the side door, facing the front, ready to go. She remembered telling him that her mother would be leaving her apartment Thursday. She was sorry for having said it, for the implied invitation, the assumption that Dan would come over then. She wanted to iron out some things without the physical closeness, to see if anything made sense without getting all stirred up, blinded to seeing anything logically.

Best not to pursue that, he thought. He drove. The cottages were dark but the other houses were lighted now as they traveled back, in reverse order past the farmhouses and into the city.

They had been through talks like this before. After each, fearing to let the harsh words and grim feelings stand, the armour of tension remain, they had softened themselves and each other with intimacy that masked their doubts and objections. But each time there were scars remaining when they left the warmth of their togetherness. There were more words to brood about and mull over in solitude, each their own, and then retreat from and manage a peace with. Each time it became more difficult to maneuver this treacherous route.

They parted that way, and Carol was alone in her apartment only a moment when the panic seized her, the same panic as before. She knew they would go on, and on, and what was impossible would seem possible for a moment, a day. And what was remote came near now in the craving of her body. She looked forward to Thursday, but a growing displeasure with herself took the edge off her anticipation. She was glad her mother was in bed.

Dan felt quite differently, as he always felt when he left Carol and his thoughts were all on facing Lois, on her knowing where he had been, on her suspecting, perhaps, he had been doing what he had not done tonight.

His eye caught the pegboard in the garage when he pulled the car in, the pegboard over the workbench, with tools and spare parts for mower and car and furnace, wiping rags neatly bagged and ready. Lois had torn them for him from old shorts and pajamas of his and from an old towel. He had an idea for adjusting the grass catcher for next spring, and seeing his tools, he looked forward to working on his car on the week-end. He would get the heater going in the garage. He settled into his possessions again and felt a comfort and ease. A good feeling of security, being surrounded by familiar and predictable inanimate things.

When he went in the side door, he heard the washer and dryer running in the basement. The water was running in the laundry tub and he heard a pail hit the side of the tub. He went up the five steps, past the kitchen, and into the bedroom. Her blue dress was laid out on the bed, the silver pendant he had bought for her beside the dress.

He was taking off his shirt when Lois came in. "Were you going somewhere?"

"*We* were," she said moving to hang up her dress. "But I did think the pendant would go well with that dress. You were sweet to get it for me." She kissed him as she picked up the pendant and put it away in the jewel box in her top dresser drawer.

He said nothing, trying to remember what it was he had forgotten, where they were going tonight. She saw this.

"Three guesses."

"I may need more."

"Well, try one. I wouldn't cut you off at one. Give the man a chance."

He sat down on the bed and put his chin in his hand. He was thinking.

Bark on the Ground

SHE WAS about nineteen in the photograph, young and beautiful and dark. Not dark brooding as in later years (though even then holding a young girl's look until the last grim days) but dark eyes and eyebrows and eyelashes and hair, a striking contrast to her white skin.

I remember her in the photograph, the family photograph, with her mother and father and sisters and brother: the parents stern, proper. I'd had it enlarged and then turned it down into the oak of the mantel until I could face the pain of her life still coursing through mine. Even with the leisured wisdom of hindsight I found nothing in her face portending the trials to come.

Now I had come here to learn about the affair, to track down the disturbing talk that mother had "chased after" LR to Detroit.

"I tried to get a job in one of the car factories," my uncle Colin is saying. "There was nothing back in Compton, no work, and we were just married. Amy and

I stayed at your mother's." He's telling what he remembers back fifty-eight years when they were in the city for their honeymoon.

I've been trying to edge my uncle to talk of mother and LR since Nancy and I arrived from the other end of a telephone wire uptown in Compton.

He said to come right down and as soon as I hung up, Nancy and I drove down the main street and turned at Prince, and there he was standing in the full summer behind the still-hanging winter storm door, looking more like a reflection than a person. Behind me were the Varleys' coleus and the geraniums I have thought about for twenty years. I never found coleus in such shaded sanctuary leafing, splashes competing, anywhere else, nor geranium leaves so pungent.

He came out only when we were going up the steps and I shook his hand, liver-spotted, wrinkled, and cold. There's a vigor in his handshake, and his face holds the same trace of a smile that I always looked for on the farm or later in his garage in town, and I never knew if he was serious or joking. We went summers, my mother and brother and I, to visit her sister Amy and her husband Colin, first on the farm, later here in town.

"Nancy, this is Uncle Colin." He takes her hand and I sense it warming then. "That's where I got my name."

When I see him or think of him there is expectancy, as if I might discover why I have his name. What did he mean to my mother? I have LR's last name, but there's no pride or expectancy there, only questions and doubts, shame even.

"Well, it's been twenty years," Colin starts again,

"since you were here last." He'll say more and we wait. We have to get used to the pauses. I go down the steps to the lawn and it's still deep like a carpet and dark green. "I held him," he's saying to Nancy, "when he was six months old."

Colin has to talk first of me as a baby and then about his trying to get a job in the car factories. I know if I push him too fast and he leaves something out of what he wants to say, he might leave something out of what I want to hear. I wait.

"We went with your mother and LR to the hospital a few times. He went in alone and would come out with a white bundle and put it in a corner of the back seat. He'd say it was a baby, dead, and he'd take it to the undertaker's place where he worked." It's quiet. He hasn't said it all.

Years later when my mother remarried, I followed both curiosity and revulsion through dresser drawers where diaphragms and jelly and applicators were hidden or readied in nightgowns. And layered down under shelf paper were old sepia-toned portraits linking a boy's hopes and fears and pride and shame to the dusted murky oval world of LR. It was always LR. He left when I was six months or so. I was three when my mother got the divorce, and nine before I knew what the initials stood for. Like my mother, I avoided talking about him.

"Come inside, it's cooler," Colin says.

This is not the sitting room I remember, a room sealed off from all time but Sundays, a room where visiting preachers sat, and recently-dusted Bibles awaited them. My uncle now lives in this room. There are snap-shots and portraits piled and scattered, and old letters. He's been living here, working on a past, rooting for something, for someone.

"If you've got a few days, why not stay? I'll drive you around to the mill and the old farm and bakery, and you can look through these pictures and papers with me."

He moves some boxes from chairs and we sit down. "Well, we always wondered, and suspected too if the truth be known, that there were no babies in those bundles. That he just went in the hospital to see that woman — she was a nurse there — and this was his ex-cuse, bringing it out and taking it to the undertaker's." Nancy nods and Colin turns more to her.

Is Colin just taking my mother's side? Can I recall now something deep somewhere in me, and only need the right connections to some remote synapse to bring that experience back? Is there a voice that comes back, or what did the car door sound like, or were there trees on the undertaker's lawn, and where did the shadows fall? Little things. I want somehow to certify, to authen-ticate all of this from somewhere deep in the marrow of my bones. To separate it from more recent memories and from the overlay of what others say, what suits them to remember.

This is the first I've heard of LR carrying bundles out of a hospital. But did I live through it? Did my eyes catch a corner of that white bundle or feel some shiver go through my mother that reverberated in my tiny bones? It does match the agony mother said she lived through, the torment of his seeing Nan, leaving us, leaving mother with her own baby, alive in her arms and not in the back seat bundled, abandoned to death.

"The soup," Colin says, jumping up and rushing out of the room. "I plumb forgot about the soup I was making." And his voice carries as he hustles to the kitchen.

"Are we staying?" Nancy whispers.

"Why not. Even if there is soup."

"Or I could go on to Sue's tomorrow, and you could stay." Her sister and family live ninety miles east.

"That would give me more time to talk to him."

Colin is soon back in the doorway. "Well, I have some soup. It's fit for the King of England." He rests his hands on the door moulding, one on each side of him. "The Queen too."

"If it's not too much bother," Nancy says. Then, getting up, "Can I help?"

"Don't fuss yourself. I'll have it ladled out in a minute." He turns and then turns back. "If you want to wash up," and he points down the hall.

There are more letters and photos in the kitchen. Colin moves some of them to make the table and three chairs clear. "Amy's been dead nine months and the place hasn't had a decent cleaning since. I've been looking at pictures and reading old letters." He moves a snapshot album. "She had cancer. I wanted to stay with her at the hospital, but of course they wouldn't stand for it. The doctor was a butcher and the nurses," and he coughs on the words making their reluctant way out with the soup going down, "they might as well have been pushing trash in a wheelbarrow as my Amy in a wheelchair."

He takes a deep breath and catches a second wind, then seeks and finds relief in turning to more recent events. He tells of chopping out the cedar hedge between his house and the Varleys' next door, how he got it all but a big and stubborn stump and hailed a town truck passing and had them hook up a chain and pull it out. He has other jobs lined up for himself: looking after a transmission valve in his old three-holed Buick, tuning the mower motor, and fixing the Varleys' eaves-trough. He will get out the long ladder for that, the thirty-foot one. No, he doesn't mind heights.

There's no anxiety or rush in any of this, no schedule to meet, just a steady succession of jobs to get ready for and work on and then talk about. "But the housework, inside things, a woman's work, gets short shrift." He uses the same wash cloth and dish towel for all the kitchen chores and for washing himself too.

The phone on the kitchen wall rings and Colin gets up and answers it. Soon he's telling the story about the hedge on the phone. Nancy clears the table and runs hot water and finds clean cloths and starts doing the dishes. I walk through the lean-to pantry and outside where the cordwood is stacked against the wall. Next spring only the bark on the ground will remain from this pile.

So, he was whoring around when I was, what, six months? And who knows how much before that. Probably when I started in the womb and grew there. More truth than ignorance in mother's thinking LR had a detachable penis. Of course she hadn't put it that way to me, the day we were painting and she told me.

Nor will I use those words later when I tell it to Colin.

We are alone together then, Colin and I, for three days when Nancy visits her sister and family. The first afternoon we sit on lawn chairs in the shade of the maple. There are thoughts forming but there is hesitation too. At first it will not be said right, but time will help to shape it better, and I wait for that. I speak first, more impatient than the uncle who has outwaited both adversaries and friends. It is slow and sparse talk at first. When I try to direct the conversation to my questions, Colin wanders back to talk of his jobs at hand.

I learn patience from this, but the questions remain. I hear him tell the story of the hedge to three different people. At first this exasperates me, that he has so many words but so few for the answers I want to hear. But then it gives me hope that Colin remembers because he rehearses so much. His memory works by imprinting events and ideas for long recall, by telling them again and again. But then, I wonder, are there other things he hasn't told anyone, secret and painful things, faded and forgotten for want of telling? Or has he brooded over them and remembers by telling them over and over to himself?

I recall my grandmother telling me about Colin and Amy. I was just a boy, perhaps ten. She talked about the money they owed her and grandfather for the farm, and never paying any of it, even when they lost the farm and had a good garage business in town. Grandma told the story a little at a time, spread out over the days. She gave from her supply of gumdrops the same way, one gumdrop each night before bedtime. Always just one, a tease to the palate and spreading out the cavities. But I was not chosen namesake of a deadbeat, surely. There had to be more to it than that.

Colin sleeps downstairs on a daybed. The upstairs room where I sleep is small and stuffy. A picture of daughter Janine, who died at age nine, rests alone on the dresser. Her dark eyes remind me of mother's and follow me to every corner of the room. The same dark eyes, the same first name. I lift the picture to turn it and notice the oasis of green wood under it and the gray desert of dust all about it. But I've turned the picture into the mirror and the eyes still follow me. Janine had my mother's name and I have her father's name. Why?

The bedroom opens to a room across the hall where Amy's green fiftieth wedding anniversary gown hangs, and other dresses. A hat and scarf and gloves lie just as she left them before going to the hospital. Amy's things up there and thoughts of her dying lend an eerie feeling to being upstairs, mysteries threatening to crowd out the mysteries I track.

I want to be within talking range of Colin as much as I can, so I move a pillow and blanket down to the couch off the dining room where Colin sleeps on his never-made-up daybed.

We talk after the lights are out at night and talk when we waken and before we get up. We talk walking uptown to the post office mornings. We talk in the shade of the house and trees afternoons, sitting in lawn chairs under spruce and maple, looking over to neighbour Hank Varley hoeing slowly in his garden and stopping to rest, winded. Hank's sick wife looks out the kitchen window and waves forlornly to Colin, as if it takes all her strength to move her pinched bony arms.

"When did you get the farm?" I ask. "It was fun going there summers as a kid."

Slowly the brooding releases to words. "I never wanted the farm," and the corners of his mouth turn down in a way I have never seen before. "That's why I wanted a job in Detroit at a car factory, looking for one on our honeymoon." He gets up and walks to the fence and leans on it, telling Varley about the hedge and the eavestrough jobs. He comes back to his chair and moves it from the edge to the center of the shade.

"I never wanted it," comes out again with no prompting but an inner urge. "I wanted the Oliver house. It's down past the bakery. I wanted to keep on carpentering. I could've paid for that house with some pigs I was raising at my folks' place. But when Amy and I got back from our honeymoon, her father, your grandfather, just went ahead and bought the farm for us, for her, a wedding present, the down payment at least. They kept paying on it because I never made any money on it, kept running me more and more into debt, a debt I never could get out from under."

I wait, wanting to put it right. "Did you, could you have told grandpa you didn't want the farm before he bought it?"

Colin looks at me. He looks away, and then, slowly, "You can't talk to people who don't talk to you to find out what you want, because they already know what's best for you."

I've heard it, not all of it, but what my uncle now

and my grandmother years ago would ration out to me, but never to each other, from their store of brooding.

I'm up early the next morning and go out to the front porch to sit. There was no air on the couch in the living room. A light breeze stirs on the porch, and the concrete slab still holds sun warmth from the previous day. Nearby crickets stop their song until I settle into a chair, and then they join the distant chorus again. A brown and white dog passes on his rounds from tree to tree. A black cat ahead of the dog's route, seeing but not seen, ducks under a parked car until the dog passes. There's a click at the door and Colin comes out.

"Too stuffy in there," he says. We sit five minutes, ten, just a word or two, the heat, the cat, and then quiet again. Then it comes. "I never told this before," and Colin shifts his chair to face the street, away from me, as if he'll tell it and I can listen but he's still not telling it to anyone.

"We used to argue, Amy and me, always about the farm, the mortgage, the burden of it, growing like the crops never growed, the crops failing, me failing. It got so bad, the arguing, one night I slept in the hayloft in the barn. I intended to take off the next morning and never tell anyone where I was. Oh, I would've written her father and told him the trouble he'd caused, the trouble I'd had and couldn't take no more. But Amy came out to the barn in the morning and told me to come in the house, just that, just come in the house and I did."

A faint glow rises from the fields beyond the road

and there are cars in the distance. The mill shift is arriving. A robin calls, and then another.

"I bet there'll be a good view of the sun rising over that field," I say, trying to lighten the mood for a moment. A door opens and closes; it's Varley next door standing on his porch in his pajamas, running his hand through his night-tossed hair.

"Varley's worried about his wife. Her heart. I was up a bit last night and looked over. He was wandering through his house, room by room." Across the fields a rooster crows.

Questions remain. "Grandma sold her house when grandpa died, and then for thirty years went from one child to another, staying several months or a year with each by turn. I wonder why she felt she had to sell her house?" There is no answer.

"Your farm was gone, and you were in town and running the garage by then, before she sold the house." I had made it a statement, thinking there would be no answer. "I remember summers there, just uptown here, watching the big trucks and tractors in for repairs. Seemed like a good business." He grunts. I think of the gumdrop days, "... never paid anything ... even with the garage business ..."

"I made three hundred dollars one year, just enough for seed, all year working, working that farm. Most years I had to borrow just to pay the interest. When the sheriff came he sat at our table for supper and cried for the little family being evicted, things piled up to be auctioned off, the sale."

"But that was the farm. What about the garage?" Colin is up by then and starting back into the house. He doesn't answer.

We go inside and dress and have breakfast. "This here's Frank Anders," he says, picking up and then putting down a snapshot without handing it to me as he appeared to be doing at first. "Toward the end Amy's mind was going, hardening of the arteries. I was taking her for a ride one day over to Bannerton, and she said, right out of nowhere, 'I should've married Frank Anders and you should've married Janine.' When we got to …"

"She meant Janine, my mother?" I interrupt.

"Yes, we were good friends all through school. Amy always said if your mother hadn't gone away to Detroit, I'd've married her eventually, then *she'd've* been on the farm. Amy and me'd kid each other about it, but at other times we were serious about it and argued, saying we were second fiddle, second choice, she to Janine and me to Frank." He turns the Anders picture over.

"Well, as I was saying, when I got to Bannerton I went into the liquor store and came out with a bottle in a bag and put on like I was going to drink it, reacting to her outburst about Frank and Janine. She straightened up and was just fine from then on until her last week, before she died, and she wasn't herself all that week. But in Bannerton that day," and Colin chuckles and looks at the snapshot again. "I never saw such a remarkable change in anyone in my life. I don't mean it was an act, but … "

"Well, yours was an act. And it snapped her out of it,

pretending you were going to drink." I smile at Colin still smiling at his Bannerton experience.

Colin turns slowly, facing me then, takes a step and seems to lean his whole weight on one finger on the table, the index finger of his right hand. The smile is gone and as he speaks each phrase comes slowly and separately. "Your mother, Amy said, someone told her, I don't know myself, understand, but someone said your mother chased to the city after LR when he moved to Detroit."

I turn from Colin as from something ugly, revolting, profaning mother's memory. "That box of pictures and papers you gave me yesterday to look at. There were two pages someone wrote, just a note about you and LR being at my grandfather's house to see my mother one evening around Christmas, and then you both left to go home. But someone went back to see my mother." I reach over and pick up two pages from a box. I turn to the bottom of the second sheet and read, "'And then in ten minutes I went back alone ...' and the next page is missing."

Colin walks to the window, loosening his collar. "I never believed it myself, her chasing after LR. But when you think what I went through with her parents – and they were her parents too – well, maybe she had a lot of cause to go to Detroit, whether LR was there or not. If she'd've stayed in Compton and married, surely she'd've got a farm, her husband would've, me or LR or who-ever." He pushes a curtain aside. "I don't know where the rumour started, where we heard it, her chasing after LR."

"I've heard it before. But the word 'chased' is away off. Now I'm going to tell you something I've never told anyone else." I wait a minute, not sure I can say it.

"My mother never had a clue about marriage or sex, let alone chasing after someone. Her uncle in Detroit arranged a job for her there in a sewing factory, and she boarded with the aunt and uncle, a minister. Those were the reasons grandpa let her go. She was there a year and LR asked her to marry him." Colin turns to look out the window, as if putting together what I am saying with something he'd heard long before.

"One time we were painting the house, this was years ago, and she was telling me about when they'd just married. She didn't want to have a baby yet. She was so young and they were poor. She said they had a sterling serving dish from the wedding but she wore the same winter coat she'd had in high school. LR had told her she didn't have to worry about a baby, that he'd 'take it out before he went off.'"

Colin seems uneasy with this and turns a chair around, but then doesn't sit down. "Mother didn't know what he meant by that. She didn't know anything. She thought he meant he'd detach it or something before he went away, 'went off.' She was young and her mother or father hadn't told her anything, she said."

Colin sits down and runs both hands through his hair.

"Mother didn't know anyone in the city except her uncle. She couldn't ask him, a minister." I turn to Colin. "Yesterday I wondered why you couldn't speak straight to my grandpa about not wanting the farm. Straight talk's painful. For me too. It's hard asking you about the missing page, and you haven't answered me. What happened?"

"I went back. Earlier, with LR there I hardly said anything, he was such a good talker. I wanted to be alone with her so I could at least talk and make a good impression. But your grandpa came in and I soon had to leave. He was very strict with her. In a year she went to Detroit. The second prize was that your mother gave you my name. I think she felt sorry for me by then."

Had Amy started the rumour? She had reasons.

I lift some papers inside the box and bury the two pages down near the bottom of the pile. "Can we go to the cemetery now?"

Colin puts a large crowbar and shovel and some rocks in the trunk of his car. In the next hour he'll bend and buckle and heave his four-score shoulders and arms to the job of raising and straightening and firming up the gravestone my mother shares with her parents and an uncle. Only then will he carry water in an old galvanized watering can to the flowers on Janine's grave, his daughter dead at nine, whose picture was duplicated nine times and placed in as many rooms in his house. He could grunt but never whine, sweat but no tears that anyone would ever see.

I walk over to mother's grave. Alone on the grass I wait, and the only sound that comes is the hand pump up and down squeaking as Colin fills the watering can.

It's been twenty years, mother, twenty years buried, laid to rest, rest at last, maybe, down into the tomb of the earth, the womb of the earth, carrying, as another saying goes, carrying your secrets to the grave. It's no secret you had enough to run from to blind you for a while to what you were running into.

A bell sounds once in the distance and I wait but it doesn't ring again.

I hear you reciting, mother, lines you told me from your schooldays: Goodland, Oxbridge, Greenmill, and Blackmoss, towns along the railroad, and then Compton. I get up from the grass and brush my hands twice across the seat of my pants.

While Colin puts the watering can back and closes the tool shed, I walk along the stone fence row where the mower doesn't reach for a clean cut. I'm bent over studying a Queen Anne's lace when he comes up and grunts, "Weeds!"

"I was going to dispute that – a flower to me, a weed to you – and then I remembered you were a farmer."

"Not a very good one, but I still rooted out the weeds."

I hold the tallest flower cupped in my hands, seeing for the first time that there's a purple centre. I look at others and they all have this purple centre. "I always thought they were pure white. How did I miss it all these years?"

"There's a good saying. 'Let sleeping dogs lie,'" Colin says, muttering "Questions, questions," as he walks to the car.

I tip the long stem of the flower toward my mother's grave and smile. I throw her a kiss across the top of the flower.

When we get back to Prince street it's almost noon, and the Meals-on-Wheels lady is there. She tells Colin they're going to take him off the program for a trial period. He seems to be doing so well, and is always "off gallivanting somewhere" anyway.

A note from Hank Varley is stuck in the door. He and his wife have been taken to the hospital. Colin is to pick the vegetables in the garden, and not forget the chives by the fence row, and enjoy them the rest of the summer because Hank knows they won't be back from the hospital.

Nancy returns in the afternoon, and when we're ready to leave I tell Colin I'll try and not stay away twenty years this time. Colin says he won't be there, he won't live out the year. I protest, trying to lighten the mood. I haven't found all the answers I came for, but some questions have softened. And then there are some things people don't ask about because, well, they just know. I don't push about when I'll see my uncle again. He talks like someone who knows.

It Could Be the Ocean

TEN OR TWELVE fishermen were spread out along the old concrete breakwater. The early arrivals had staked out claims on the few green wooden benches, sitting beside their tackle boxes and lunch pails. Others sat on camp stools or stood up casting their bait into the river. I noticed the woman at once, coming from her car in the parking lot, and going along the line of fishermen, talking to some for a minute or two, but passing on after only a few words to others.

I caught the purpose of her mission before she got to me, and it gave me time to think of a story to tell her. Perhaps her elfish-looking Chihuahua provided some impulse, or perhaps it was an attempt to vie with the Queen in *Alice in Wonderland*, thinking of six impossible things before breakfast. Or it might simply have been that I wanted to give her more of a response than the grunts and stares or few dull words she was getting from the others. I thought she needed more than grim cold facts.

It happened along the river, but I kept thinking it could have been the ocean. It was because of Francine that I thought of the ocean: sunrise over the Atlantic, along the Atlantic City boardwalk with the gambling casinos as a backdrop, and the mystery of whether it was suicide or homicide over a gambling debt. Or, it could have been the Pacific, a dramatic sunset along the Big Sur coast south of San Francisco, involving a visitor to the Tassajara Zen Mountain Centre, a frightening walk through the Ventana wilderness, and finally a questioning of participants at the Esalen hot baths, with the Santa Lucia mountain range as backdrop.

Had it happened at the more glamorous Atlantic City or Big Sur, I think my wife Francine *would* have investigated, walked around and talked to people who might have been witnesses. But I'm not convinced she would have walked along the more prosaic waterfront of the Detroit River, as this widow walked, asking fishermen if they'd seen her husband a week earlier.

"My husband died here last Sunday," she said when she got to me. "I'm just trying to find out what happened."

"I'm sorry," I said.

"Oh, he expected it ... heart attack. He'd had two before that, a year apart, the last in November."

Two lake freighters exchanged whistle blasts and a small cabin cruiser echoed them with its higher whistle and passed between them. Two young girls in bathing suits on the cruiser waved to crew members along the rail of one freighter.

"Your husband was a fine man." I looked into her

eyes. There seemed no sadness there, only a seeking. I had thought of saying that her husband had almost landed a record-sized fish and saved a boy from falling into the river. But I backed away, deciding to stay on safer, less dramatic ground. "Did you get his fishing gear?"

"Oh, he wasn't fishing. He never fished."

"The dog ..." I started to say, and I looked down at the little Chihuahua on the too-heavy chain she held. I planned to tell her that the dog raced around the picnic tables and the man enjoyed chasing it and then putting it back on the leash. I thought she needed details, some specifics to make the scene come alive.

"Oh, Penny wasn't with him."

"Well, there was a dog, I thought, I mean ..." I was mumbling now, my confidence eroding. "I'm sorry, I guess I wasn't very observant. It must have been another time." I had been looking down at the dog, as if talking to it until I could get my story straight. I looked at her again. "But I'm sure your husband was a very good man, and it's too bad." By then I wasn't so sure he *was* a fine man, or if *she* thought so. I had garbled everything else. Maybe I had that wrong too.

"Someone called the emergency medical," and she turned to look at the phone booth by the refreshment stand.

Two fishermen got up to tend their lines, taking their rods out of cracks in the breakwater concrete, tugging, reeling in a bit, then putting the rods down again and adjusting the bells on the lines so they could wander about or nap and not have to watch the lines every minute. They put their jackets on the back of the bench, jackets that had kept them warm earlier but now were shed in the warming sun.

"I think many of the same fishermen come here every Sunday," I said, trying to encourage her to keep looking, asking. The grunts and few words of the others didn't seem so callous now compared to what I had said.

"They don't say much. Afraid, perhaps, of saying the wrong thing." She looked back at me, and I shuffled my feet.

"What do you think happened?" I asked, really wanting to ask her what it was she wanted to hear, but that would have been too obvious. This was a necessary task for her, but necessary for *what*? Had they argued Sunday morning and he'd come to the river to cool off? If he wasn't fishing or walking the dog, what *was* he doing? Did she go to church Sunday mornings, and this was his outing, or out? I'd received no confirmation when I said he was a fine man. She might have thought him mean and ugly but couldn't abandon someone who'd had two heart attacks. Or she might have worshipped him and regretted not being with him every minute of the days left to him before another attack.

"From what I've been able to piece together," she started, and then walked over to a tree with the dog. I waited. A fisherman emptied the few remaining drops of coffee from his thermos, coffee he'd probably nursed along and hoarded by sipping through the early morning cold, but now the refreshment stand was open and he went over for a refill.

I thought of Francine again. We hadn't been getting along at all well lately. What held us together? There was tension when we were together and relief when we were apart, and yet we kept coming back to fight. If something happened to me, Francine would never go out inquiring as this lady does, I thought. She'd take what money there was, yell "yippee" and head out west. It's not all one-sided; to be fair, I'd probably do the same, going east.

A fisherman passed between us, and she turned to him. "Excuse me, mister, my husband had a heart attack here last Sunday. I'm looking for someone who saw him, who could tell me anything." She kept talking, warding off the possibility of yet another one who could tell her nothing. "I was just wondering if you ..." and she looked away.

"The man in the red jacket?"

"Yes, yes ..." Here was someone who knew. She waited.

"It was over there, on that bench. He went there, holding his chest, bent over. At first no one paid too much attention. You know, we're all pretty independent here. We talk, but if someone wants to be left alone, we don't bother him. That's the nice thing about this place." He was talking carefully, still not saying much about her husband.

"How long did he sit there? Did he take his pill?"

"He stayed there, kind of slumped on the bench," and the fisherman moved toward the bench a few steps. "There was a bottle on the other end of the bench and somehow he knocked it off and when it smashed a couple of us looked over again and he was doubled up. My buddy and I went over to him and another guy then went to the phone over there and called emergency. My buddy's not here today," and he looked around, "and I don't see the guy who made the call."

The woman's dog barked its shrill bark when two boys rode near with their bicycles. She pulled the dog closer to her feet.

"The medics pulled right in here. Drove right over the grass. Backed right up to the bench and put your husband on a stretcher and drove off, one of them connecting up oxygen, red lights flashing and you could hear the siren for about five minutes. The police came a bit after that and talked and took some names and got your husband's cap. I hope you got it."

"Yes, they came to my house. I went to the hospital but he was dead before they got him to emergency." The woman thanked us and walked back to her car. She didn't talk to anyone else. She had heard what she came for, or heard enough to put an end to asking for more. She would live and die with that. I felt like a fool for trying to concoct some story, something elaborately false when the truth was so starkly simple. She would flesh out the gaps and questions remaining with her own details. Perhaps she had done that all through the week, and the simple facts of the actual scene now blended in with the picture she already had.

On the way home from the riverfront I resolved to learn a lesson from the widow and her husband's heart attack, to be kinder to Francine, to use the days I hoped we had yet, showing my love and appreciation, getting along, not waiting until it would be too late. I could say that coincidentally my wife, Francine, was dead when I got home and so there was nothing I could do to put my resolve into action, that it was too late. I could say that I went around to the neighbours asking what had happened, the details of the accident, what Francine said, who called the ambulance. And I could say that in my mind I began forming the words of a fine eulogy.

But Francine was still very much alive and kicking, kicking verbal brickbats at me, and I kicked my share too. We went on like that. There's no use denying it or trying to think up six impossibilities before breakfast, or even after lunch, of what could have happened but didn't.

We're still together and I go to the riverfront every week or so. I think of the woman and her Chihuahua and her husband in the red jacket. I never sit on "his" bench, but I look over at it and then I look out on the river and think that Francine and I must be lucky, lucky to be alive, lucky we haven't had heart attacks. I know that much. And I stand there trying to think of other lucky things. I know there must be some, but, just keeping to the facts, I have trouble thinking what they are.

Mona

"WHO'S MONA?" My wife was putting two slices in the toaster.

"Mona? Mona who?" I asked.

"That was *my* question."

"Oh, *Mona*." I must have sounded evasive, but I wasn't completely awake. I remembered then. Mona. It was part of my project in working with my dreams.

"You were talking in your sleep last night," she said.

"I was talking into my recorder, some things from a dream. I'm not writing them down anymore. I can't read my writing in the morning."

"And Mona was in a dream." She waited. Then, "Who's Mona?"

I tried to explain lucid dreaming, being aware that you're dreaming, and then taking an active role in the dream for working out any problems. I had to record my dream as soon as I wakened.

I'd tried writing dreams down, but found that invariably I couldn't read the scribbling the next morning.

"lbcnrt fcy pqwm." But what does it say? And what does it mean? In the night – or was it 3 am? – it seemed so important, even urgent, to get it down so it wouldn't be lost. But when the light of the next day came, my message was still in the dark. Maybe the "b" and "l" were transposed, or the "c" was really an "o", but what does *that* make, and where do I go from there?

Even some legible items made no sense when they faced the light of the next day. *Helmut Kohl's helmet, monkey's ring tail, contact him.* Contact *who*?

So, I gave up night writing and started to use the small tape recorder under my pillow. The problem was that my wife invariably wakened with my dictating, and this in time inhibited my speaking beyond a whisper. Then she found the whispers easier to hear than the muffled voice. I was defeating my purpose in not being able to record everything of a dream, lest it waken her. And I could hardly deny whatever she heard, for the voice was my voice and the words were my words. Like Mona.

There is something very private about nighttime messages and I didn't want to be inhibited from recording everything, no matter how it might raise up guilt or ambition, lust or greed. And so there were questions raised, "Who is Mona?" for example. Not about climbs up the Alps, even the southern slope, or talking to the Ayatollah, or hang gliding over Toronto. But who is Mona?

I tried abbreviating my messages, using what I thought were key words instead of speaking in sentences. But the words, even when individually decipherable, made no sense when strung together. *Lamb's wool, longitudinal, thrifty, hub caps* – these did not inspire coherent action. Or any action at all, for that matter.

And then I focused on the content in short phrases and the messages came through loud and clear but were hopelessly simplistic. *Listen and empathize, one step at a time, continue to hope.* Is that all? What did I leave out? The answer must be more complex than that. Where's the high tech? Where the experts? Where the fancy jargon? At least it should sound impressive, or what's a dream for? I could do as well awake.

I no longer save undeciphered nighttime notes or tapes, hoping time and repetition will force them to yield their secret. I suspect there's a code somewhere and I'm not yet privy to it. I'd like to get it settled though. If I'm not going to get help with the great Canadian novel, I might as well just sleep on and enjoy mountain climbs and hang gliding. And Mona.

But I do wish I'd recorded more of the dream about Mona last night. I've never been to Paris but she looked just like her picture. She told me some secret. Something about her smile. I wish I'd got it on tape.

Born in Detroit, Michigan, Stewart Moore attended Wayne State University, where he earned degrees in philosophy, psychology, and social work. While attending Wayne State, he won the Tompkins Award for poetry. In his lifetime, he worked at a variety of jobs: as a welder, factory assembly-line worker, maintenance repairman, secretary, store clerk, real estate salesman, carpenter, landscape gardener, summer resort operator, soldier, minister, social worker, and finally, as a Professor in the School of Social Work at the University of Windsor. In 1992 he earned the Teaching Award of the Ontario Confederation of University Faculty Associations. He wrote throughout his life, publishing sixteen articles in professional journals, three short stories in literary magazines, four articles in books, one film, and three books: *Over the Hill to the Moorehouse, Dandelions Have Their Own Gold Standard*, and *For Nought/Mr. Mankind: Two One-Act Plays*.

CRANBERRY TREE PRESS

*This book was set in 12-point Bembo, which was
modelled on typefaces cut by Francesco Griffo in 1495.
The typeface was designed by the Monotype Corporation
in 1929 under the supervision of Stanley Morrison.*

The paper is Rolland opaque lisse crème 120 M.

The book was designed by David Langs.

*The book was printed and bound by
AGMV Marquis, Montreal, Quebec, Canada.*

Also by Stewart Moore

Dandelions Have Their Own Gold Standard

Poetry and prose about go-go gods, unbreakable soldiers, marble angels, battles, today's witch, and the surf, the deer, and the gulls: lines gleaned when apprenticed to life and taught by death.

For Nought / Mr. Mankind: Two One-Act Plays

For Nought – One man's struggle to fathom the pain and suffering that first erode his faith and then become a part of it.

Mr. Mankind – The war crimes trial of a follower who pulled the trigger and dropped the bomb. "The tyrants of war would have died in obscurity had it not been for the followers."

Over the Hill to the Moorehouse

The author's account of three years spent in the north woods. Building a cabin and living lean to life without telephone, electric lights or running water. An inner odyssey in quest of a simpler, ecologically sound life. Pump and pail and outhouse share pages with the call of loon and owl and whippoorwill.